D1236728

VANISHING SWEETNESS
A GINGERBREAD
MYSTERY LOVE STORY
BY: JAMES BREZNICKY

Table of contents

Chapter One

A cockle-warming track to reel in the festive season, complete with sleigh bells which delivered the distinctive jiggle to mark the beginning of the festive season. The air was chilling and whisked the falling snowflakes haphazardly. Some were struggling to trudge through the thick layers of snow just to get to a nearby shelter, while others; like Mr Muller, were fixing his mailbox, completely unfazed by the semi-chaotic weather conditions.

The candy canes driven into different spots on the ground littered the scenery. Some children were running around in the snow making snow angels, while others were picking the solid candy rocks scattered along the ground. One of the gingerbread children stopped and looked up at a large sign which read;

Welcome to the North Pole.

After gawking for a few seconds a snowball rammed the back of his head, pushing it forward as he was snapped back to reality, he fetched some snow from the ground and chased after his friends.

Candland was always booming with life during the Christmas season, its location was still

5

somewhat like a mystery to the inhabitants of the town all they knew was that it was far away from any other civilization. It was a small, quaint little town with cobblestone streets lined with colorful gingerbread houses and candy canes. Every home was uniquely crafted, with different shapes and sizes, and decorated with colorful icing and edible decorations.

The town was a paradise for children, with an abundant supply of sweets and treats to go around. On Christmas morning, the town would be filled with laughter and cheers as children run around with winter coats and scarves wrapped around their necks to protect them from the winter. Every door would be adorned with holly and even the snowflakes that fell from the sky, which seemed to be made of sugar.

The Town of Candland Was a place of wonder and enchantment, where the spirit of Christmas was alive and well.

In the cozy house, a family was getting ready for the Christmas season. From the delicious scent of gingerbread and candy filling the air, it was clear that something special was happening.

At the center of the activity was a young gingerbread man named Jack. He had been lovingly crafted by the family and was excited to take part in all the festivities. He was wearing a bright red bowtie and a little Santa cap. He couldn't help but smile as he looked around the house, which was made entirely of candy. The walls were made of peppermint and the furniture was made of licorice. Even the floor was made of gumdrops!

The family was busy decorating the house, hanging garlands of candy canes and strings of sweet-smelling orange and cinnamon. Jack watched as his family members laughed and sang, dancing around the house and enjoying the Christmas spirit.

Soon enough, it was time for the family to have dinner. He eagerly took his place at the table with the rest of the family, marveling at all the delicious food. As they dug into their meal, he couldn't help but feel overwhelmed with joy. He was part of a happy family and they were all celebrating the Christmas season in a house made of candy. What more could a gingerbread boy ask for?

Love.

Jack's mom always said he was made with the freshest of ingredients, and he was always full of energy. He loved to explore and try new things, but he was always careful not to wander too far from the gingerbread house because of the recent happenings.

After he was done eating, he dabbed his lips with a napkin to get rid of the food stains and got on his feet. He headed towards the hallway and began packing his skiing gear. "You're not going ice-skating are you?" Miranda, his mother, asked.

"I am."

Her expression morphed into one filled with concern. "It's snowing heavily. I don't think it's safe. Plus, you know it's not quite safe out there." He sighed with a weak smile, "Relax, I'll be careful. Besides, the snowfall has reduced, look!" He gesticulated with his arms towards the window. She sighed and shook her head in defeat while her husband Victor snaked his hands around her waist to calm her down. "You know there's no stopping him when he grabs that skiing gear," he joked.

"See you later!" Jack said in a sing-song manner as he jogged away from the house and shut the door closed.

He reached the park and began walking in with a sense of anticipation. He'd been looking forward to this all week- a chance to go ice skating in the snow. Feeling the chilling winter air rush over his face. He zipped up his coat and pulled on his woolen hat, glad to be out and about on such a beautiful day. He had decided to go ice skating, a rare pleasure in these days of ever-increasing temperatures and less snow.

It was a cold winter day, with a light snow still falling. He breathed in the crisp air and smiled. He loved the feeling of being outside in the winter.

He walked over to the lake and saw that the ice was freshly groomed and the snow still on it was sparkling in the sun. He put on his skates and began to make his way onto the ice. He glided over the surface with ease, the cold air and snowflakes making him feel exhilarated. For a while he felt like he was flying, the only sound was the swish of his skates against the ice. He spun and twirled, feeling the joy of being able to move and be free.

But then, suddenly, he felt himself slipping. He tried to grab onto something, anything, to stop himself, but it was too late. He fell, hitting his shoulder and part of his head against the ice. Instantly he felt a sharp pain, followed by an intense throbbing. He laid there for a few moments, trying to get his bearings, but then the pain became even more intense and he felt nauseous. He knew he had to get help.

He attempted to drag himself off the ice but a loud yelp escaped from his throat as he fell back down in pain. "Are you okay?" A soft voice called as she rushed towards him.

She flashed in and out of his vision as he blinked his eyes before he finally blacked out, her face being the last thing he registered. When he regained his consciousness he was in a room that was mostly white. He tried to look around but it seemed he was alone, until he noticed Miranda dozing off by the corner.

He tried to sit in an erect position, propping his body against his arms as he did so, all the movements and shifting of the bed awakened Miranda. "You're awake, the doctor said you should get some rest," she said. "Why what happened?"

"You had a concussion after your fall," she said in a reprimanding tone. He knew better than to push the topic any further. "There was a girl…"

"She's the one that brought you to the hospital, she left some minutes ago."

He slouched his back against the backrest and sighed.

Chapter Two

The next morning came like a haze, even though Miranda insisted that Jack stayed home and rested, he protested, claiming he was completely fine and had recovered from the concussion. So, like every other normal day, he headed straight for his morning shift.

Life in Candland was quite satisfactory for Jack. Every day started off with a fresh batch of butter bread, cookies, and other assorted pastries being baked in the local bakery. He would scurry over to the bakery each morning and help the baker mix and roll out the dough, cut it into shapes, and carefully place it in the oven.

Once the pastries were done baking, Jack would help the baker to decorate them. He quickly adds little icing details and colorful candies to each cookie. He took great pride in his work and was always sure to make each treat extra special.

The sun shone brightly through the windows of the bake shop, its rays casting a warm, inviting light over the rows of tantalizing treats displayed in the glass case. As the door opened, a gust of fresh air blew past the warm air that had been present for hours.

A young woman, most likely in her early twenties, walked in. He snapped his head back to face her when he caught a glimpse of her face. She was the most beautiful girl he had ever seen, with her sweet smile and her beautiful curly light brown hair. Jack was immediately smitten. She took a deep breath, savoring the scent of freshly baked goods and the sound of laughter coming from the café tables. She adjusted the straps of her bag and stepped further into the shop. As she made her way to the counter, her eyes drifted over the pastries and cakes.

Her mouth was already watering at the smell of freshly baked bread. She glanced around, taking in the rows of breads and pastries, the comfortable chairs, and the smell of chocolate. She was just about to make her selection when her eyes fell on Jack.

She smiled as she noticed a tall, handsome apprentice standing near the register, helping customers order. He had a kind face and a warm smile, and the girl couldn't help but feel drawn to him. As she made her way to the register, she realized who he was.

"Hi good morning," her voice rang cheerfully. He scrunched his eyebrows as he struggled to pinpoint the familiarity of the face. "You're the one that rescued me at the ice-skating park," he said, without breaking eye contact. She smiled, "Yes, sorry I couldn't stay longer till when you regained consciousness, I really had to get home."

"It's okay, we still met didn't we?" They both chuckled.

She ordered her treats and waited, her eyes never leaving Jack's frame. She noticed his dark eyes and the way his hair brushed lightly against his forehead. She felt her cheeks flush and her heart flutter. If she wasn't brown her cheeks would have been as bright as freshly plucked tomatoes.

He finished helping some other customers and turned to her. He smiled; she felt her heart leap in her chest.

He quickly averted his gaze, feeling a little embarrassed for being caught staring. He made his way over to the counter, trying to appear nonchalant and not thinking too much about the woman. He ordered a loaf of bread and waited while the baker wrapped it up, stealing glances at the woman out of the corner of his eye.

When his bread was ready, he made his way over to the woman. He cleared his throat and asked her if she needed any help carrying her purchases. She smiled and thanked him, and the man felt a flush of warmth spread through his body. "By the way, I didn't get the name," he said while she was collecting her order.

"Amelia, how about you?"

"Jack."

"Hope you're fully recovered from that concussion?" She asked. He smiled weakly and rubbed the back of his head, "of course. We should hang out sometime, get to know each other," he proposed in an attempt to divert the flow of the conversation. "Sure."

"Ice skating park later tonight maybe around 6?" He said with a mischievous glint in his voice. She snickered, "6 it is."

She flashed a warm smile at him before exiting the shop with her goods. Shortly after she left, his best friend Gregory entered the bake shop.

Gregory walked into the bake shop with a spring in his step. He had something to tell the waiter, and he was sure it would be something he'd never forget.

He looked around the shop and noticed that the shelves were nearly empty. He figured it must have been a slow day. He spotted the worker.

Who was usually working in the back and approached him with apprehensiveness.

"Hey, Gregory, how's it going?" Jack asked with a smile.

Gregory looked up from the counter, making sure to look both ways before responding. "Hey, have you heard about what happened in town?"

Jack nodded slowly as a crease formed on his forehead. Gregory took a deep breath, and then let it out slowly. "Mrs. Muller is missing."

Jack looked intrigued. "Oh, do you think it has any relation to the recent mysterious disappearances?"

Gregory nodded. "I'm hundred percent sure it does, something funky is happening in town, Jack. I heard she went missing after she went for a jog with her dog. The dog made it back, but it was traumatized."

Jack's eyes widened in surprise. "Three people have gone missing in the last week alone. The police don't have any leads and it's really worrying everyone."

Gregory furrowed his brow. "That's really scary. Do the police have any clues or suspects?" Jack shook his head. "Not yet. There have been no witnesses or any evidence left behind. It's like the kidnappers are ghosts, disappearing without a trace."

Gregory sighed. "It's so frustrating. I mean, what can we do? We can't just sit here and do nothing. We have to do something to help."

"No, we don't," Jack said with finality in his tone.

Gregory ignored his disposition and continued, "I've been thinking of setting up a neighborhood watch. We can organize our own patrols and try to keep an eye out for suspicious activity. We might even be able to catch the kidnappers if we stay vigilant."

"Have fun getting kidnapped or killed too."

Gregory scoffed; he went ahead to make an order.

Jack was always trying to keep him in check with his sweet tooth, but Gregory never listened. He was always ordering something sugary from the shop, and this day was no different.

Gregory had already ordered a slice of lemon meringue pie, a strawberry crumble, and a chocolate eclair. He was about to order another sweet treat when Jack warned him to stop. He said, "Gregory, you know you are diabetic. I'm worried you'll get sick from eating all these treats."

But Gregory was determined. He wanted to try the new raspberry tart the shop had just released. He ordered it, and his friend shook his head. He said, "I guess I can't stop you, but at least be careful okay?"

Gregory nodded and took a big bite of the tart. He had never tasted something so delicious before. He was in heaven, and he couldn't help but order more treats. His friend just sighed and shook his head.

When he was finally done, he thanked his friend for all the warnings. He said, "I know I have a sweet tooth, but it's all part of the fun!" His friend just rolled his eyes and said, "Just don't do it too often, okay?"

Gregory smiled and agreed. He would take his friend's advice and try to be more mindful of his sweet tooth. With that, he waved goodbye and headed out of the bake shop.

Gregory was made from almond flour, as his creator had chosen to make him sugarless. He was a diabetic, so sugar was not an option, but he never listened. His body was light brown and slightly crumbly, but his shape was perfect, with a round head, arms, and legs. He had two small eyes and a wide smile, a simple and classic gingerbread man.

Soon the day was over and Jack had closed his shift, he was excited to meet Amelia at the ice-skating park. He finished wiping down the counters and washing the last of the dishes from the day's orders at the bake shop. He had been working hard in the kitchen all morning, but now he was free to go.

He quickly changed out of his apron and into his black jeans, a navy-blue sweater, and a black wool coat. He quickly ran a brush through his wavy brown hair and applied a light layer of cologne.

As he stepped outside, he felt a sudden rush of excitement. The sun was setting and the sky was illuminated with a warm orange hue. He grabbed his skates and walked to the ice-skating park which wasn't too far away from the bake shop.

The cold winter air blew through the park, causing the man to shiver. He pulled his coat tighter around him and kept his eyes on the ice-skating rink ahead of him. It was a beautiful sight; dozens of people gliding around the ice in a flurry of vibrant colors, their laughter and chatter ringing through the air. The lights twinkled in the trees, a sign to attest to the festive season.

The man smiled as he walked closer to the rink. He had been looking forward to this moment all day. He had pictured him and Amelia on a romantic evening of ice skating, and he was excited to finally see her. He scanned the crowd, searching for her face.

Finally, he spotted her. She was wearing a warm coat and matching scarf, her face glowing with happiness as she skated. He couldn't help but smile as he watched her, her graceful movements making her seem like a swan on the ice.

The man slowly made his way to the rink, his heart filled with joy and anticipation. Soon, he was standing right beside her. She was wearing a bright red coat and a matching scarf, and she had a warm smile on her face. She waved at him, and he waved back, eagerly making his way over to her.

He flashed a warm smile her way as they instinctively began to walk towards the bench.

"Wow, this ice-skating park is beautiful in the evening," he remarked. She nodded her head with folded arms, "mhmn, it sure is. Look at the trees! They look so ethereal."

"You're right. It's like we're in a snow globe!"

"I know, it's so romantic."

The both of them busted out in short laughter. "You know what else is romantic? Ice-skating with you."

"Well, aren't you a sweet talker? By the way, hope you're good?" He sighed, suddenly realizing she was talking the same motherly tone as Miranda.

"I'm fine, let's go."

"Alright, let's do it."

He began to lace his skates up. He took a deep breath, feeling the crisp winter air in his lungs, and got on his feet. Amelia was still struggling to fix hers but she eventually finished and was met with his extended arm to provide her with support. She grabbed his arm and stepped onto the ice-skating rink, his arm was around her waist to keep her from slipping backwards. She looked up at him with a mix of excitement and apprehension.

"Are you sure about this?" she asked.

He smiled reassuringly and gave her a gentle squeeze. "Trust me, you'll be fine," he said.

She nervously stepped onto the ice and immediately began to wobble. He put his arm around her waist and held her steady, helping her balance.

"It's like walking, but on ice," he said, his voice calm and soothing.

She took a few more steps, and he could tell she was starting to get the hang of it. He chuckled as she began to move a bit faster, her movements becoming more confident.

"See, you're getting it!" he said, his voice filled with pride.

But then she stumbled and stumbled again, falling onto her back. He quickly moved to help her up, but she just lay there, laughing.

"I guess I'm still a bit of a rookie," she said, her eyes twinkling.

He smiled and pulled her up. "That's alright," he said, giving her a kiss on the forehead. "We'll just take it slow." An awkward silence lingered between them as they just stared at each other, unsure of what the gesture meant.

He scratched the back of his head and looked away, "I'm sorry," he said, avoiding eye contact. "It's fine," she said in a soft tone while trying to hold back a snicker.

He held her close as they continued around the rink, her confidence growing with each step. With his help, she was soon skating like a pro, her face bright with joy.

As they glided around the rink, Jack knew he'd made the right choice in bringing her here. He had a feeling she would be a natural.

He could feel the energy of the other skaters as he weaved and glided across the ice. He felt like he was flying and the movements felt almost effortless. As he passed the other skaters, he noticed some of them smiling and waving at him. He smiled back, feeling a sense of belonging and joy.

He and Amelia locked hands and moved in near-perfect synchronization around the rink. They spent the next few hours skating around, talking, and laughing. Jack couldn't believe how well their conversation flowed, and he felt himself growing more and more attracted to her with every minute that passed.

"We should get going, it's getting really dark," she pointed out. Jack looked around as if in disbelief of what she had just said. Deep down he didn't want this to end, so quickly. They sat on the bench and began to unlatch their skiing gear.

A woman ran towards the rink screaming hysterically. "They took my son! My son!" People began to gather around while a few tried to get her to calm down.

The area was filled with frantic energy, as the woman paced back and forth, her hands shaking and her voice trembling with fear. She mumbled prayers under her breath as she pulled her long, dark hair away from her face and held it in her hands. Her face was pale, her eyes red and swollen from crying.

"We were just by one of the entrances of the park! It all happened so… so fast, they took him!" She screamed as she tried to clench the ground with her palms. "Who? What happened mam?" A lady yelled and lowered herself to the ground.

The woman struggled to speak, her voice was shaky and the fear was still evident. "It happened in a flash; I didn't see it. Something just took him! Like, like an ambush." She broke down and fell to the ground, crying her heart out.

Incessant whispers broke within the small on-looking crowd. Amelie and Jack shared a look, and he instinctively pulled her towards him in a protective manner. The woman's voice rose hysterically in the humid night air. "My son! He's gone!!" She frantically scanned the faces of the crowd that had gathered around her in a circle, her eyes wild and desperate.

The feeling of fear and apprehension rippled through the crowd like a shockwave. People began to whisper between themselves, their voices edged with worry. Someone suggested calling the police, but the woman shook her head, her eyes still searching the faces around her. "No! He's out there somewhere!"

The crowd grew uneasy, their fear increasing as the woman's panic grew. Everyone began to worry about their own safety and security, wondering if this could happen to their own children.

The woman continued to search the faces around her, her voice trembling with emotion. "My son, please! Anyone! Has anyone seen him? Please, I'm begging you!"

The crowd stood in silence, their fear and apprehension growing as the woman's panic increased. No one had seen her son, and they all feared the worst.

She stopped her pacing and looked around the room, her eyes darting from one corner to the next. She felt so helpless, so lost. Tears streamed down her face as she began to sob uncontrollably.

The sound of the police sirens became audible as they were approaching the park. "We should get going," he suggested. She nodded in agreement and they began to make their way to the entrance.

"Candland is getting very unsafe with the mysterious kidnappings," she said as she rubbed her arms to rid herself of the cold.

Some police cars whisked past them and the blue and red light from the ambulance cast itself against their skin. "I'll accompany you home."

"Thank you," Amelia said.

They walked slowly down the street, the streetlights offering the only illumination in the dark night. Jack glanced around nervously, his hand hovering protectively around Amelie's shoulder.

"You sure you're alright with me walking you home?" Jack said, his voice low and guarded.

Amelia smiled, looking up at him with a reassuring expression. "I'm sure. I really appreciate you doing this. It's nice to have someone looking out for me."

Jack smiled back, and the two of them continued walking in silence, the only sound being the distant hooting of an owl.

When they reached Amelia's front door, Jack hesitated, not wanting to leave her alone.

"Thank you for walking me home," Amelia said, her voice gentle and sincere. "It means a lot."

Jack nodded, taking a deep breath before speaking. "I just want you to be safe, Amelie. I care about you and I don't want anything bad to happen to you."

Amelie smiled, her eyes filling with emotion. She reached out and brushed his cheek with her fingertips. "I know, and I-" Her front door was yanked open.

A plump, beautiful figure stepped out. Her dark eyes were inquisitive and her gaze was directed at the two. She wore an apron around her ample waist, and her hair was tied back in a neat bun.

"Ah, I see you have company Amelia," the woman said. Her voice was polite but firm.

Jack stepped back, embarrassed at being caught in the moment. Amelia blushed, and Jack smiled nervously.

"We were just talking Mom," she said sheepishly.

The woman nodded; her gaze still inquisitive. "It's getting late," she said. "You should both come inside now, wouldn't your friend like to have some dinner?"

"Oh no I really should get going I don't want to intrude-"

"Nonsense! Come have dinner," she insisted.

Jack stepped into the house. Amelia showed him to the dinner table, where her family was already seated. He sat down, feeling even more uncomfortable.

The conversation was a bit strained at first but gradually eased into a more natural exchange. Jack noticed that Amelia seemed to be watching him closely as if she was gauging his reaction to her family.

"What's your name again?" Rodolfo, Amelia's dad said. "Jack," he mumbled. "What do you do?" Amelia's mother, Sarah, coughed. "Rodolf..." she cautioned..

Jack lowered his head and intensified his gaze on his food. "I work shifts in a bake shop." Rodolfo scoffed. They continued to dine in awkward silence.

When dinner was over, Jack thanked Amelia's family for the meal and said he had to get going. He thanked Amelia for inviting him, but he could tell she was disappointed.

When he got home, he went straight to his bedroom upstairs to get a good night's rest.

Chapter Three

Gregory arrived at the meeting spot early in the morning. The morning chill was making him shiver a bit. He had a clipboard in one hand, and a cup of hot cocoa in the other.

He looked around at the small gathering of neighbors. They were all bundled up in coats and hats, and they all seemed a little apprehensive.

Gregory greeted them all warmly and cleared his throat. "Thank you all for coming. I'm sure you've heard about the mysterious disappearances in the neighborhood. I wanted to get together with you all to discuss what can be done to keep our neighborhood safe."

The neighbors all looked a bit uncomfortable, but they agreed to discuss the issue. After a few moments of awkward silence, someone spoke up. "Maybe we should start a neighborhood watch?"

This suggestion was met with a murmur of agreement from the rest of the group. Gregory smiled and nodded. "That's a great idea. I was actually thinking the exact same thing."

He proceeded to explain the roles that he had assigned to each person. Some would be patrolling the streets at night, others would be keeping an eye on suspicious people and activity, and some would be responsible for gathering information. He emphasized the importance of working together and staying vigilant. He also made it clear that anyone who saw anything suspicious should alert the others immediately.

When he was finished, he thanked the group for their attention and asked them to disperse to complete their assigned tasks. As the members of the neighborhood watch dispersed, Gregory felt a sense of relief knowing that they were doing all that they could to protect their community.

Jack awoke to the sun streaming through the window, but he had a heavy feeling in his stomach. Today, like another weekday, he had to go in to work the bakery shift. He got ready for the day.

He rushed into the kitchen of his family's home and quickly grabbed a plate of pancakes, eggs, and bacon from the stove and plopped down at the kitchen table. His mom and dad were already sitting there, chatting about the upcoming Christmas Eve festivities.

"Hey, Jack!" His little brother said.

"Hey buddy, sorry I'm late," Jack said as he shoveled a forkful of pancakes into his mouth.

"No problem, we were just talking about who's going to be in charge of the Christmas lights this year," Miranda said.

Jack swallowed his food and said, "I'm sure you guys can figure it out without me, I gotta get to work soon." He shoveled in the rest of his food and grabbed a banana to eat on the way to the bake shop.

When Jack got to the bake shop, his boss was standing by the door with folded arms, giving him a stern look. "You're late, Jack. You know I don't tolerate lateness," his boss said.

Jack nodded and quickly apologized before grabbing his apron and setting to work. He knew he was going to have to work extra hard to make up for his tardiness.

When he entered the bake shop, there was already a line of customers waiting. As he opened the doors to the shop, the customers began to chatter about something that had happened in the neighborhood.

"Did you hear about Mrs. Muller?" one of the customers asked.

"What about her?" asked another.

"She's disappeared," the first customer said.

Jack was intrigued by the conversation and began to eavesdrop.

"Disappeared? How?"

"No one knows. She was last seen a few days ago, but no one has seen her since. It's so strange. Just last night a little boy was snatched from his mother as well," the man said with a hint of grief in his tone.

Mrs. Muller had been such a beloved member of the neighborhood. She was always so kind and generous, a direct opposite of her husband. He couldn't imagine what could have happened to her, he thought about what Gregory had told him earlier as well, Mr. Muller was really missing.

The customers continued to talk as Jack did his best to serve them. He couldn't help but feel uneasy. He knew that something was wrong in Candland but he couldn't put his finger on it.

The rest of the day went by in a blur. By the time Jack had finished his shift, the conversation about Mrs. Muller had died down. He couldn't help but feel a tug of sadness as he left the bakery.

It was a foggy, chilling evening as Jack walked home from work. He wrapped his coat tightly around himself, trying to shield himself from the cold. His thoughts drifted back to the dinner party at Amelia's house from the night before. He had enjoyed himself, but it was clear that there was some tension between him and Amelia. He couldn't quite put his finger on it, but he couldn't shake off the feeling that something was off.

As he trudged down the quiet street, he heard the sound of barking in the distance. As he got closer, he saw a figure walking a group of dogs. As he got closer, he recognized the figure as Amelia, a woman he had met the night before at the dinner party.

"Jack! I didn't expect to see you out here," Amelia said as she approached him, her voice sounding a bit surprised.

"Yeah, just walking home from work," Jack replied, trying to shake off the chill from the night air.

"I'm sorry about how dinner went last night. I know it got a bit tense," Amelia said, looking down at the dogs, her voice sounding apologetic.

"No worries, it's all good," Jack said, brushing it off, trying to sound casual and nonchalant.

They chatted for a bit, and it was obvious to both of them that they were attracted to each other, but they were in denial. The conversation was easy, and they laughed and joked, but there was a sense of hesitation and awkwardness between them.

"Can I walk you home?" Jack asked, finally breaking the silence.

"No, it's okay, I'll be fine with the dogs," Amelia said, a hint of sadness in her voice.

"Well, I'll see you around," Jack said, feeling a bit disappointed.

"Yeah, see you," Amelia said, as she continued on her walk with the dogs. Jack watched her disappear into the fog, wondering if he had missed his chance. He couldn't shake the feeling that something had changed between them, and he couldn't help but wonder if he would ever have another opportunity to make things right.

As he walked home that night, he couldn't help but feel a sense of dread. He had a feeling that something bad was about to happen.

Amelia had just finished her evening walk with her dogs when she felt a cool breeze blow. She could feel the hair on the back of her neck standing up as a chill ran down her spine. Her heart began to race as she quickly realized that something was not right. She took to her heels, running as fast as she could, her dogs barking frantically beside her as they ran along, she wanted to reach her house as quickly as possible.

The force seemed to be closing in on her, and Amelia could feel her heart pounding in her chest. The rustling of leaves grew nearer and nearer and she panned her vision both ways in search of the source of the noise. She kept running, her heart pounding in her ears, her breath coming in short gasps.

The trees were alive with the sounds of rustling leaves and creaking branches, a barely visible figure could be seen descending from the treetops. It was difficult to make out any distinct features, but the figure seemed to be shrouded in a lustrous glow that made it hard to look at directly. Amelia caught a glimpse of the figure and tried to outrun it, but it was too close.

Amelia could feel her heart pounding in her chest and could see time pause as the figure descended lower and lower. She saw the eerie shimmer of the light that seemed to surround the figure. Her dog, a small golden retriever, yipped excitedly, not yet sensing the danger. Suddenly, the figure swooped down towards the dog.

The dog, startled by the sudden movement, yelped in fear and tried to run, but the figure was too fast. In a blur of motion, the figure scooped up the dog in its arms and disappeared back into the canopy, leaving behind nothing but the screams of the dog lingering painfully in the air.

Amelia could hear her dog's frantic barking fading away into the distance.

One of her dogs had just been caught, and Amelia's heart broke as she heard its yelp of pain. She didn't have time to think, and she kept running, her feet pounding against the pavement. She could see her house in the distance, and she knew that she had to make it there safely.

Finally, she reached her front door and quickly unlocked it. She slammed it shut behind her, her heart racing. She was safe, but she was scared. She couldn't stop thinking about what had just happened, and she knew that she would never forget the eerie feeling of the sinister force that had tried to attack her and her dogs. She hugged her remaining dog, trying to calm down and make sense of what had just happened, tears streaming down her face. She knew she had to tell someone, but she was too scared to speak, too scared to even move from where she was standing. She felt like a prey, caught in a trap and she didn't know how to get out.

Her parents rushed out of their rooms. "Amelia what happened!?" Her mother Sarah asked, her voice laced with concern. Amelia said nothing but crawled into her parents' embrace.

Chapter Four

Jack slowly opened his eyes as the morning sun streamed through the window. He stretched his arms above his head and let out a contented sigh. He laid there for a moment, taking in the familiar surroundings of his room. He glanced at the clock on his nightstand, it read 7:00 am. He remembered he had planned to get an early start on the day, he had to meet Gregory later in the morning, it was a Saturday and today his shift at the bake shop was in the evening.

He slowly sat up in bed and swung his legs over the edge. He sat there for a moment, rubbing the sleep from his eyes, before standing up and making his way to the bathroom. He splashed some water on his face and looked at himself in the mirror. He had a big day ahead and he needed to be fresh. He brushed his teeth and took a quick shower, feeling the warm water invigorate him.

He went to his room and picked out his clothes for the day. He decided on a casual outfit, a comfortable T-shirt, and jeans. He got dressed and made his way to the kitchen. He put on a pot of coffee and sat down at the table to wait for it to brew. He heard the sound of his phone buzzing on the counter, he got up to check it, it was a message from his friend confirming their meeting point.

"And just where are you going, Jack?" Miranda questioned.

As he sipped his coffee, forcibly then smacked the base of the cup against the table. "To city park to see Greg."

"You're supposed to help with the Christmas lights…"

"Love you, bye." He hurriedly grabbed his backpack and headed out the door.

It was a cold Saturday morning and Jack was on his way to the park to meet his friend, Gregory. As he walked through the park, he saw Gregory sitting on a bench, bundled up in a warm coat, scarf, and gloves. Jack made his way over to the bench and sat down next to his friend.

"Hey, Greg, how's it going?" Jack asked, rubbing his hands together to warm them up.

"Hey, Jack. Not too bad, just trying to keep warm on this chilly morning," Gregory replied with a smile.

"I heard on the news that temperatures are very low." Gregory nodded in confirmation, "at least they can make snow angels," he said as he pointed with his nose at some kids who were making snow angels and rolling on the ground. As they were talking, a group of children ran past them, laughing and playing. One of the kids, a little boy, stopped right in front of them, staring up at Jack with big brown eyes.

"Hi, mister!" the boy exclaimed, with a big grin on his face.

Jack smiled back at the boy. "Hi there! What's your name?"

"My name is Timmy," the boy replied, still smiling.

Gregory chuckled. "Well, Timmy, what are you and your friends up to today?"

"We're playing cops and robbers!" Timmy exclaimed, his eyes lighting up with excitement.

Jack and Gregory exchanged a glance and grinned at each other. "Well, that sounds like a lot of fun," Jack said, ruffling the boy's hair.

"Yeah, it is! I'm the best robber," Timmy said, with a note of pride in his voice.

"Well, I hope the cops catch you," Gregory said, with a chuckle.

Timmy grinned and ran off to join his friends, leaving Jack and Gregory to continue their conversation.

Jack's smile slowly faded as he watched the boy play. "What's wrong?" Gregory asked. "A woman's son went missing in a park too, I'm pretty sure he'd be around this kid's age."

An uneasy silence followed.

After a while, Gregory turned to Jack and said, "Hey, I wanted to tell you about something. I've been working with the neighborhood watch recently. We've been trying to keep the area safe and secure, especially with the holiday season coming up."

Jack was intrigued. "Really? Isn't this like the job of the police? Doesn't sound safe to me."

"Well, we've been keeping an eye out for suspicious activity, making sure that everyone's homes are secure, and working with the local police to keep the area safe," Gregory explained.

Just as Gregory finished speaking, his phone rang. He pulled it out of his pocket and answered it. Jack could see the concern etched on Gregory's face as he listened to the person on the other end of the line.

"What's wrong, Greg?" Jack asked, sensing something was not right.

"They said someone was attacked yesterday," Gregory said, his voice heavy with worry. "Last night on her way home with her dogs. She's okay but shaken up. She's the first person to survive an attack other than that boy's mother; their statements would be very important in helping us figure this out."

Jack's heart sank, "you said last night? With dogs?" He couldn't help but feel worried because the description matched Amelia's. "Y-yeah why?"

His eyes widened, "it might be Amelia, I have to go check on her." He jumped on his feet, and Gregory followed after him, still half confused.

Jack and Gregory crouched behind a thick bush adjacent to Amelia's house. The bushes rustled and crackled beneath them as they shifted their weight, trying to catch a glimpse of Amelia through the windows, making sure they stayed hidden. Jack knew Amelia's father, Rodolfo, didn't like him and he probably would not hesitate to call the police if he saw Jack loitering around his house. The scent of freshly cut grass and blooming flowers filled the air, but it was overshadowed by the musky smell of the damp earth they were sitting on.

"Are you sure this is a good idea, man?" Jack's friend whispered urgently. "We could get in a lot of trouble if we're caught."

"I just have to make sure she's okay," Jack replied, his voice trembling with anxiety. Gregory sighed, "Why didn't you ever tell me about her?" He asked in a whisper. 'I just met her some days ago," Jack defended. "*Some days* is a really long time."

"Shhh I'm just worried about her. Plus, we can talk about this later. I don't wanna get caught here."

They peered through the leaves, scanning the windows for any sign of movement. Suddenly, Amelia appeared in the living room, sitting on the couch, and staring blankly at the TV. "See, she's fine," Gregory said, trying to reassure him.

But Jack wasn't satisfied. "I need to talk to her and make sure she's really okay," he said, and before his friend could stop him, he stood up and walked towards Amelia's front door, making sure to stay hidden from Rodolfo's view. The crunching of leaves and twigs beneath his feet was the only sound he could hear, his heart was pounding in his chest, his palms were sweaty, and his stomach was filled with knots.

His friend followed, calling out to him, "Jack, what are you doing? Come back! This is crazy!"

But Jack was determined. He stood by the window, waving his arm at her until he caught her attention. His heart was racing, his mind was processing all the possibilities of what would happen if Rodolfo caught him. Amelia looked his way with an arched eyebrow. She dropped the book she was holding and looked both ways before moving towards the door. She opened it and stepped out. "Jack, what are you doing here? Is everything okay?" she asked.

Jack breathed a sigh of relief. "Yeah, I just wanted to make sure you were okay," he said. "I heard you got attached." Amelia smiled nervously. "I'm fine, Jack. I promise. I just miss my dog."

Relief flooded his being upon hearing those words, "sorry about the dog… and for showing up unannounced like this," he said. "I should get going."

She stretched her neck to look over his shoulders. "Is that your friend in the thicket?" He turned around and cussed under his breath, he shooed him away with hand gestures and turned back to face her. "Yes, don't mind him, I'll be on my way."

"You sure you don't wanna come in?" She asked. "No, don't worry, it's good."

"It's because of my dad isn't it?"

He snickered nervously and began taking steps back. "I'll see you around."

Jack and his friend left, feeling relieved that Amelia was fine. "I told you she was fine," his friend said as they walked away.

"Yeah, I know," Jack replied. "But I needed to make sure for myself, just in case." Gregory groaned.

Amelia closed the doors gently as turned around; a chill ran down her spine when she noticed Rodolfo's figure by the stairs. He was staring deep into her eyes with folded arms. She cleared her throat and lowered her gaze. "Who was there?" He asked. "No one, I thought I heard something." He cocked his head slightly to the side, "are you sure?" He questioned, slowly making his final descent from the last step. She nodded.

He opened the main door and stuck his head outside, scanning the area with his eyes. He turned back to look at Amelia. "Alright, you know we have to be extra careful after what happened to you." She offered a weak smile and made her way to her room.

His eyes followed her retreating back until she was out of sight then he looked back at the door. He felt something was off but didn't bother to press any further.

Jack opened the door to his home; he walked into the living room and was greeted by the sight of some Christmas decorations hung on the walls. The tree was up, and it was covered in lights and ornaments. The mantel was lined with stockings, each with the name of a family member written in glitter.

Tim was sitting on the couch, playing with a remote-controlled car. He looked up as Jack entered the room. "Hey, Jack. Check it out, Mom and Dad started decorating for Christmas," Tim said with a grin.

Jack groaned. "Great. Just what I need, more decorations."

Tim's grin faded. "What's wrong? Don't you like Christmas decorations?"

Jack sighed. "It's not that. It's just that every year, our annoying cousins, and family members come to stay for the holidays and drive me crazy. They always eat all the good food, hog the TV, and never clean up after themselves."

Tim nodded in understanding. "Yeah, I know what you mean. But at least they're family, right?"

Their father, Victor, walked into the room and overheard their conversation. He chuckled. "Oh, come on, boys. Lighten up. It's the holidays. Time to be nice to your family, no matter how annoying, or loud they are."

Their mother, Miranda, walked in and scolded them. "Victor, don't encourage them. And boys, your father is right. Family is family. We may not always like them, but we should always show them love and kindness."

Jack rolled his eyes but knew his mother was right. He took a deep breath and decided to try and make the best of it. "Fine, fine. I'll try to be nicer. But if they start driving me crazy, I'm not responsible for my actions."

Miranda smiled at him. "I know you'll do your best, dear. Now, let's go help your father finish decorating."

Jack groaned again, knowing he could not escape this time. He followed his parents and brother to the living room to help decorate for Christmas. Despite his initial reluctance, he found himself getting into the holiday spirit. He helped his father put up the lights on the tree, and his mother helped him hang the ornaments. Tim was in charge of the tinsel and was having a blast throwing it everywhere.

As they were finishing up the decorations, the doorbell rang. They all shared a look, and the silent debate on who was to get the door ensued. With a sigh, Jack headed to the Hallway. He opened the door and the face of Sussie, their next-door neighbor came into view. "Hello," she said in a pitchy voice.

Sussie was a neighbor whom much to everyone else's knowledge had a huge crush on Jack. She was standing on his front porch. She shifted nervously from foot to foot, her eyes avoiding him. Jack couldn't help but notice the way

Sussie's hair was styled, the way her sweater clung to her figure, and the way she kept glancing at him shyly. He knew Sussie had a crush on him and wondered if she took this extra measure to look good for him. "Hey Jack," she said, her voice barely above a whisper.

"Hey Sussie," Jack replied, trying to hide the confusion in his voice. They had never had an awkward interaction before, and he didn't know what to make of it.

Just then, Miranda came up behind him. "Sussie, dear! How lovely to see you," she said, her voice warm and welcoming.

Sussie's face relaxed into a smile and she stepped forward, hugging Miranda tightly. "Hi Mrs. Thompson," she said.

Miranda stepped back and gestured for Sussie to come inside. "Please, come in. We were just about to have some hot cocoa; would you like to join us?"

"We were?" Tim asked. "Yes," she responded dryly.

Sussie nodded eagerly and followed Miranda and Jack into the living room. Once they were seated, Sussie took a deep breath and turned to Miranda. "I actually came over to talk to you and Jack about something," she said.

"Oh?" Miranda prompted; her eyebrows raised in curiosity.

"My parents want to host a Christmas Eve party in our backyard, and we were wondering if you and Jack would like to come?" Sussie asked, her eyes flickering between Jack and Miranda.

Jack could see the subtle flirting in Sussie's eyes and the way she kept trying to catch his gaze. He didn't know how to handle the situation and felt a bit trapped.

Miranda's face lit up with excitement. "Oh, that sounds like so much fun! Of course, we'll come. Thank you for inviting us, Sussie," she said.

Jack nodded his agreement, still feeling a bit bewildered by the turn of events. "Great! I'll let my parents know you're coming," Sussie said, standing up to leave. "Thanks again for having me over."

Miranda hugged Sussie goodbye and Jack walked her to the door. As she stepped out onto the porch, she turned to him with a small smile. "See you at the party, Jack," she said.

Jack nodded. "See you at the party," he echoed, as he closed the door behind her. He let out a sigh of relief and went back to join his mother, wondering how he was going to deal with Sussie's crush at the Christmas Eve party.

Chapter Five

The next day came quickly, Jack was glad today wasn't an off day, else he'd have to be the one to deal with his annoying extended family when they'd arrive. He quickly got ready for work and dashed out of the house, if he played his cards right he wouldn't need to even interact with anyone if he came home late enough because they'd all be fast asleep. That was his plan.

When he got to the bake shop he quickly retrieved his apron from the wall and tied the rope around his waist to keep it in place. His manager briefly peeped in on what he was doing in the kitchen before heading to his office while his co-workers started attending to the customers.

Jack nervously fumbled with his apron as he arranged freshly baked pastries in the display case. It was a slow day at the bakery, and he welcomed the chance to daydream about Amelia, he hoped she would become a regular customer. Just then, she walked into the bake shop. The bell situated just above the door did its characteristic jiggle to announce the entrance of another customer. For a second, it was as if his heart skipped a beat.

"Hi Jack," she said with a smile as she approached the counter. "I'm in the mood for something sweet. Can you recommend something?"

"Of course!" Jack exclaimed, trying to sound confident. He quickly prepared a cream cup, drizzled with chocolate syrup, and topped with a cherry. "This is my special creation, just for you."

Amelia took a bite, and her eyes lit up. "Wow, this is amazing! You're such a talented baker, Jack."

"Thank you," he replied. She stained the corner of her lips with cream and Jack quickly noticed. "You got something..." he gestured with his fingers, pointing to the same spot on his own face. She was still a bit confused so he reached out and cleaned it by swiping his thumb pads against her skin. It sent a sudden sensation down her neck and she looked into his eyes. They stared at each other longer than they would both like to admit until she coughed.

"Don't you have work right now?" She questioned with a crease on her forehead. He shook his head, "it's my lunch break," he said, sounding like he was out of breath as he dragged a chair near her table.

She nodded subtly and continued with her dessert.

Amelia looked up and smiled. "How's it going?"

"It's going great. I'm glad you're here, this is the perfect way to spend my lunch break." Her eyes widened, "watching me eat?" She said in a lighthearted tone. He chuckled, "No, spending time with you, and of course watching you eat as well." He said in a husky tone.

Amelia blushed, her cheeks turning a light shade of pink.

As they continued to chat, Jack's nerves began to calm. He was in heaven, feeling a connection with Amelia that he had never felt before. He was getting up the nerve to ask her out when his boss called him over.

"Jack, I need to speak with you for a moment," his boss said, motioning him to follow.

Jack's heart sank. He was so close to asking Amelia out, but now his moment had been ruined. He looked back at Amelia, hoping she would understand.

"I'm sorry, Amelia. Duty calls. Can we continue this later?" Jack asked, trying to hide his disappointment.

Amelia smiled, her eyes sparkling. "Of course. I'll be here."

Jack followed his boss to a corner of the bake shop. "You know my rule about bringing your friends here?"

"But it's my lunch break-"

"No buts, I don't want all your friends coming here to hang around and distract you from working, for all I know you might even be giving them free food. I don't want to repeat this again, after your shift you can hang out with whoever you want to hang out with, heck Liam would even treat you like a customer, but not right now okay?"

Jack nodded stiffly and his manager walked back into his office. He walked back to the table he had just left.

"Jack, are you okay?" Amelia asked, noticing his change in demeanor.

"I can't really talk to the customers so I'm going to the back to complete the rest of my lunch break," Jack explained, feeling a knot form in his stomach.

Amelia's face fell. "Oh, that's too bad. I was really looking forward to getting to know you better."

"Me too, Amelia. But I promise, as soon as I get back, I'll take you out on the most amazing date you've ever been on," Jack said, with determination in his voice.

Amelia smiled, her eyes shining with hope. "I can't wait." She slipped a piece of paper towards his end of the table, "call me," she whispered and then walked away.

As Jack said goodbye to Amelia and walked out of the café, he couldn't help but feel a sense of loss. He was going to miss her, but he knew he would be back soon and their connection would only grow stronger.

Jack reluctantly returned to the kitchen; his mood dampened. His co-worker, Liam, teased him about his obvious crush on Amelia. "She's out of your league, man," Liam said with a smirk. Jack scoffed.

Finally, Jack's shift was over, and he clocked out, eager to call Amelia. He stepped out into the chilling night winter breeze. He tugged against his coat in an attempt to use it to wrap his body, with his gaze low and his steps brisk, Jack made his way home.

A harsh bright light penetrated painfully into his eyes, he tried to block it with his palms. He looked ahead to find a car speeding towards him. Frozen in shock, the only thing he could do was subconsciously brace himself for impact. It screeched to a stop and its caramel tires left a sugary melted trail on the ground. A man opened the door on the driver's side and slowly alighted, putting one foot out first before the other. Rodolfo came out of the car.

"Hi there Jack," he said in a low mocking tone. Jack clenched his jaws tightly in response. Rodolfo's fake smile quickly faded, "Look here punk, I don't want a lowlife like you getting with my princess got it? Rodolfo was met with silence. "Stay. Away. From. My. Daughter," he stressed, making sure to sound as intimidating as he could.

Jack remained mute, only letting his eyes appreciate the beauty of the pavement floor. Amelia's father eyed him from the crown of his head to the soul of his feet under pure scrutiny. He wore a slightly disgusted look on his face. Just as he turned around to leave, Jack finally spoke. "I really like Amelia," he muttered, infuriating the already irritated man. Rodolfo stepped closer and grabbed his collar, drawing Jack's frame into his. "I don't care, you stay away from her if you know what's good for you."

He pushed Jack backwards and scoffed, then turned around and entered his vehicle. His eyes never trailed off the young man until he ignited his engine and drove off. Jack stood there, drilled to the ground as he was trying to process what had just happened.

By the time he got home, a slight sense of relief overwhelmed him, finally, he would be getting a good day's rest. His heart sank when he caught sight of the black minivan parked in their frontage. He knew it was probably one of their annoying cousins and other equally annoying extended family members.. Sure enough when Victor opened the door, it was their cousin, Billy, and his family.

He walked in and greeted everyone with a big smile on his face, a forced smile. Just like his mother said, he was trying to be nice. His uncle Steve sat by the corner while his wife, Lisa, sat on the couch and complained about how cold it was outside. His cousin had already started their loud chattering and his grandma was being the typical judgmental old lady she's used to being. He could tell because she was harassing Miranda and Victor as usual. Some other family members were in the kitchen.

Jack felt his patience starting to wear thin. He excused himself and went to his room, closing the door behind him. He laid down on his bed and closed his eyes, trying to calm down. He knew his mother was right, family was family, but it was hard to be nice when they were driving him crazy.

He heard a knock on his door and his mother's voice. "Jack, honey, are you okay? You looked a bit upset."

Jack sat up and opened the door. "I'm fine, Mom. Just a little stressed, that's all."

Miranda smiled and hugged him. "I know it can be hard, but remember, they're family. And we should always show them love and kindness. Jack rolled his eyes and sank into his pillow.

Chapter Six

The argument between Rodolfo and Sarah had been escalating for what felt like hours now. It had started off small, a disagreement about something mundane, but it had quickly spiraled out of control.

With each word, each accusation, each insult, the temperature in the living room rose. Amelia had been watching in horror from the sidelines. She wanted to intervene, to make them stop, but she was too scared of the anger she saw in her parent's eyes.

"You're making things so difficult Sarah!" He yelled. Sarah scoffed bitterly and whipped her head around to face him, "Me? Me?! I can't believe this!" She yelled back, throwing her arms in the air to express her disbelief.

Finally, Amelia had had enough. She had quietly snuck away to her bedroom, locking the door behind her. She wanted to be as far away from the argument as possible and she wanted to try to forget what she had just heard.

But Amelia's mind was racing. She hated seeing her parents fight like this, it scared her. She was so shaken up that she decided to reach out to the one person who could make her feel better, which was Jack.

Amelia quickly sent him a text, asking if they could meet up. She needed to get away from her parents and the tension in the house, and she knew that Jack was her only chance.

Meanwhile, back in the living room, Sarah had stormed to her bedroom while Rodolfo went to the cellar. Amelia's phone buzzed, she stretched and grabbed it from her nightstand, then swiped it open.

Jack: What's up? - 7:18pm

She began typing and deleting routinely until she came to a resolve on the perfect response.

Can we meet up? -7:19pm

Jack: Now? -7:19pm

Yes if that's okay though, I just want to talk.

Jack: Alright just tell me where -7:20pm.

She relayed details about where their meeting point would be and quickly got changed into a pair of blue jeans and a hoodie to protect her from the chilly night. She made sure to stuff her bed with pillows and covered it with a blanket such that anyone that peeped into her room would think that she was in bed sleeping. She opened her room and tiptoed downstairs, making sure to stay clear of her parents' watchful eyes. She saw her dad by the cellar, drowning himself in alcohol. This was the perfect moment; nobody would realize she was missing. She let out a sigh of relief as she made it outside and into the cool night air.

She walked quickly to the park, her heart pounding in her chest. When she arrived, she saw Jack waiting for her on a bench, his face lit up with a smile as soon as he saw her.

"Hey, you made it," he said, as she sat down next to him.

"Of course, I needed to see you," Amelia said, her voice shaking slightly.

"What's wrong?" Jack asked concern etched on his face.

"Just a fight with my parents," Amelia replied, shrugging it off.

"I'm sorry," Jack said, putting an arm around her.

"It's okay," Amelia said, leaning into him. "I just needed to get away."

They sat in silence for a few minutes, taking comfort in each other's presence. Then, Jack turned to face her and took her hand.

"Amelia, there's something I need to tell you," he said, his voice serious.

"What is it?" Amelia asked, her heart pounding.

"I love you, Amelia," Jack said, his eyes never leaving hers. "I have for a long time now. I know it's fast and maybe even a little crazy, but I can't help how I feel."

Amelia felt like the air had been knocked out of her. She had suspected that Jack might have feelings for her, but she had never dared to hope that he loved her.

"Jack, I-I don't know what to say," she stammered.

"You don't have to say anything," Jack said, a small smile playing at the corners of his mouth. "I just needed to tell you. I'll wait for as long as it takes for you to feel the same way."

Amelia felt tears prick at the corners of her eyes. She had never felt so happy and scared at the same time.

"Jack, I do love you," she said, her voice shaking with emotion. "I love you more than I ever thought was possible. But my parents will never accept us being together, especially my dad."

"I don't care about that," Jack said, with determination in his voice. "I'll do anything to be with you, Amelia. Anything."

Amelia felt a warmth spread through her, knowing that Jack loved her enough to fight for their relationship.

"I'll do my best to make them understand," she said, her voice firm. "But it might take time. Are you okay with that?"

"Of course," Jack said, smiling at her. "I'll wait for as long as it takes."

They sat in silence for a few more minutes, lost in their own thoughts. Then, Jack leaned down and pressed his lips to hers, sending shivers down her spine.

"I love you, Amelia," he whispered, as he pulled away.

Jack and Amelia had just left the park after their secret rendezvous, making their way back to her home. As they walked, Jack couldn't help but feel a sense of nervousness and guilt. He knew how much trouble Amelia could get into if she was caught sneaking out to meet him.

"Are you sure it's safe for you to climb that tree?" Jack asked as they approached her house.

"I've done it a million times," Amelia reassured him with a smile. "It's the only way for me to get back into my room without anyone noticing."

Jack was still unsure, but he trusted Amelia's judgment. He wondered what type of adventures would require her to be so used to climbing into her room through the tree.

When they finally arrived at her house, Amelia explained the plan to Jack in more detail. "There's a big oak tree in the backyard that I use to get into my room," she said. "It's not too difficult to climb, but you have to be quiet."

Jack nodded, his nerves starting to settle a bit. He watched as Amelia started to climb the tree, her movements graceful and sure. She was like a cat, effortlessly navigating her way up the branches. Jack felt a sense of awe as he watched her, thinking that she was one of the bravest and most amazing people he knew.

When she finally made it to the branch outside her window, Amelia looked down at Jack and smiled. "I made it," she whispered, giving him a nod.

"You did great," Jack whispered back, smiling with pride.

Amelia disappeared into her room, and Jack let out a sigh of relief. He was grateful that she had made it back safely, and he couldn't help but feel a sense of excitement for the next time they could be together.

As he made his way back home, Jack couldn't help but reflect on the night's events. He had been so caught up in the thrill of sneaking around and spending time with Amelia that he hadn't considered the potential consequences. He made a mental note to be more careful in the future, knowing that what they were doing was risky.

But even with the risk, Jack couldn't help but feel grateful for their time together. Amelia was one of the few people in his life who truly understood him, and he cherished their moments together.

When he arrived back at his own home, Jack went straight to bed, exhausted but also feeling a sense of excitement for the next time he and Amelia could be together. He drifted off to sleep, dreaming of their next adventure.

Gregory walked down the quiet streets of his neighborhood, accompanied by four other members of the Neighborhood Watch. It was night time and the only sounds that filled the air were the crickets chirping and the occasional dog barking in the distance. Gregory carried a flashlight and a walkie-talkie, ready to respond to any emergency.

They approached a dark alley and Gregory stopped the group. "Stay here," he whispered. "I'll check it out. This part of town isn't too safe."

He walked down the alley, shining his flashlight on the dumpsters and the walls. He saw a figure moving in the shadows and quickly approached it. "Freeze! Show your hands!" he yelled.

The figure stepped out of the shadows, revealing a young man with a backpack. "Whoa, man, I'm just looking for my lost cat," the man said, raising his hands.

Gregory relaxed his grip on the flashlight and nodded. "Alright, just be careful. This neighborhood isn't safe at night, especially with... you know, the mysterious kidnappings."

The young man gave a slight nod in response and left the alley, and Gregory rejoined the group. "All clear," he said into the walkie-talkie.

They continued their patrol, checking the parks and the playgrounds for any signs of trouble. They came across a group of teenagers drinking and smoking behind a basketball court. As Gregory approached them, shining his flashlight in their faces. One of the guys was downing a bottle of eggnog, his throat throbbing as he swallowed its alcoholic content. Others were gathered around a table sniffing powdered sugar to get themselves high.

"What are you kids doing here? You know this is against the law," he said sternly. The guy cleaned the corner of his lips with his sleeves and got on his feet, "what's it to ya pops?"

Snickers broke among the group at the back who still continued to drink. "You're drinking alcohol, it's bad for your health, plus this is underage drinking."

A girl with a Mohawk scoffed from the back, "What do you know about health? You're shaped like a donut." Their cackling intensified, and they began to whisper among each other, making side jabs at his plus-sized physic. Gregory knew he couldn't handle them with normal dialogue, he let out a frustrated sigh.

"I'm calling the cops right now," he muttered and reached into his back pockets to retrieve his phone. "The police don't scare us!" One of them yelled.

"Yeah! I'm not even 18 yet, they can't arrest me!" Gregory met with the brat's bloodshot eyes and looked him square in the eye, "we'll see."

He already had the police department on speed dial so it only took a matter of seconds for him to put the call through. "Damn, he's not playing," one of the boys whispered. Confusion set among the group as they contemplated their options.

"Hello, is this the local police department?" A tiny voice screeched a response from the other end. Gregory nodded, "Okay, this is the neighborhood watch, we'd like to report something, some teenagers are behind the basketball court doing drugs." He waited for a while to listen to whoever was on the other line.

"Okay yes, it's behind city park, yes greenwood street."

"Yo, let's bounce!" One of them yelled. Only a few could get away, the majority of them had gotten intoxicated due to the effects of the eggnog. They staggered at a pathetically slow pace away from Gregory and his group.

The teenagers grumbled and tossed their cigarettes. Gregory watched them go and didn't try to stop them, he looked back at his team. "Should we?"

"Nah the police would find them; they can't get too far."

One of the women there scoffed, "Can't wait to tell Margret her son sniffs sugar to get a sugar high. The look on her face would be.." she composed herself when she realized that they sent questionable glares her way.

"What? She's the one always acting like Mrs perfect." She threw her hands in the air in surrender.

"Alright, let's go home, we've done our best for today," Gregory concluded. "What about them?" A woman said as she pointed to some of the teenagers who had fallen to the ground. "I'll stay till the police come, the rest of you can leave," he said. They all seemed to be on board with the plan, nobody wanted their night cut any shorter than it already was.

Just as some were about to start leaving, they heard a loud crash coming from a nearby house. They all shared a look and Gregory immediately ran to the house, followed by the other members of the Neighborhood Watch, he blew his whistle relentlessly as they approached.

They found the front door broken open and Gregory cautiously enters the house, his flashlight leading the way. The feeling of apprehensiveness creeped along their spine, but their strength in numbers did provide a sense of security.

From the corner of his eyes, he saw a man in the compound, holding a laptop and a sac that was presumably filled with valuables.

The man looked up and saw Gregory, he jumped over the short fence and made a run for it. Gregory went after the man, but Jasmine, who was the most athletic in the group, was quickly ahead of them and gaining on the thief.

She lunged forward and wrapped her arms around the thief's frame, throwing her weight against him and tackling him to the ground. Before he could react, other members had quickly caught up with the man. The other members of the Neighborhood Watch quickly alerted the police, who arrived within minutes to arrest the intruder.

As the intruder was taken away in handcuffs, Gregory looked at the grateful homeowner and nodded. "Just doing our job," he says.

The Neighborhood Watch continues its patrol until dawn, keeping its community safe and secure. Gregory feels a sense of pride and satisfaction as he walks home, knowing that he has made a difference in his neighborhood, even though the mystery of the random disappearances is still unknown.

Chapter Seven

Jack woke up early that morning, his usual routine when he worked at the bakeshop. He lived close by and walked to work, taking in the peaceful, quiet streets before the city started to stir. As he approached the bakeshop, he could smell the freshly baked bread and pastries, the scent a comforting one that always put a smile on his face.

As he clocked in, he said good morning to the other bakers, who were already hard at work preparing for the day ahead. Jack grabbed his apron and headed over to his station. He had been working at the bakeshop for just over a year now, starting as a trainee and working his way up to becoming one of the lead bakers. He loved the work, the smell of fresh dough, the sound of the mixer, and the satisfaction of pulling a perfectly baked loaf of bread out of the oven.

As he was rolling out the dough for croissants, his phone buzzed. He quickly washed his hands and reached for his phone, a text from Amelia. She was asking if he wanted to hang out later that day. Jack smiled, he hadn't seen or talked to Amelia after their last interaction and was looking forward to catching up.

Just then, Jack's manager, Mr Brown, called him over. Jack's heart sank, had he made a mistake? He quickly dried his hands and walked over to him, feeling a little nervous. Mr Brown was known for being strict but fair and Jack was proud of the work he did and didn't want to disappoint him.

"Jack, I need to talk to you for a moment," he said, his tone serious." Of course, Mr Brown. Is everything okay?" Jack asked, his nerves getting the best of him.

"Yes, everything is fine. I just wanted to let you know that the bakeshop will be closing for the Christmas break. We'll be closed from tomorrow until after New Year's Day," he said, giving him a warm smile.

Jack was a little taken aback. He had heard rumors from Liam and his other coworkers that the bakeshop might close for the holidays but he didn't think it would be so soon. He quickly did the math in his head; he had planned on working as much as he could over the holiday to save up some extra money.

"I see. I guess I'll have to make other arrangements for the holidays then," Jack said, trying to hide his disappointment.

"Don't worry, Jack. You'll still be paid for the days you would have worked and I wanted to give you your last pay for the year," Mr Brown said, handing him an envelope.

Jack opened the envelope and was pleasantly surprised to see a bonus check in addition to his regular pay. He was grateful for the extra money and was even more appreciative of Mr. Brown for thinking of him.

"Thank you. I really appreciate this," Jack said, smiling.

"You deserve it, Jack. You've been a great asset to the bakeshop and I know you'll continue to do great things," the manager said, patting him on the shoulder.

Jack went back to his station, still a little in shock but also feeling grateful. He thought about what he would do with the extra money, maybe treat himself to something nice or save it for a rainy day.

As he continued to work, his thoughts drifted to Amelia. He was looking forward to hanging out with her later.

Gregory entered the bakeshop, and the smell of freshly baked bread and cakes wafted into his nostrils. He glanced around the store, taking in the sight of the colorful display of pastries and treats. He spotted his best friend Jack at the counter, chatting with a customer. Smiling to himself, Gregory made his way towards Jack.

Jack noticed him and waved him over, finishing up his conversation with the customer.

"Hey there, Gregory!" Jack said with a wide grin, his eyes sparkling with excitement.

"Hey Jack, it's great to see you!" Gregory replied, giving his friend a quick handshake. "So, what's up?"

"Oh, you know, just working and trying to save some money," Jack said with a laugh. "What about you? How's life treating you?"

Gregory smiled. "I'm doing okay. I've been busy with work, but I'm managing."

Jack paused, to process the words he had just heard. "Work? You got a job?" Gregory nodded, "I'm working as an intern at the police station."

"When did this happen?"

"This afternoon, the inspector put in some word for me after the whole thing yesterday and now I'm free to resume Monday morning,"

"That's great to hear. So, what can I get for you today?"

Gregory glanced at the display of pastries and treats. "Hmmm, how about a chocolate cake?"

Jack sighed; I hope you're checking your blood sugar?"

"Of course, I am!' Gregory defended.

With an eye roll and a slight scoff, he reached into the show glass to retrieve a small chocolate cake. "So you still haven't told me about that Amelia girl we went to see the other day," Gregory said in an inquisitive tone.

"It's complicated... I like her."

Gregory raised an eyebrow, intrigued. "Really? Tell me more about her."

"Well, she comes in here frequently to buy pastries and we've been texting a lot lately. I can't stop thinking about her smile and how she lights up the room when she walks in." Jack's voice was filled with admiration.

Gregory chuckled. "Sounds like you're head over heels for her, man. What are you going to do about it?"

Jack took a deep breath, his eyes lighting up with determination. "I'm going to ask her out on a date. I just need to work up the nerve."

"I have no doubt you'll do great," Gregory said encouragingly. "Just be yourself and let her see how great you are. And in the meantime, let's enjoy these smoothies you've made."

Jack handed Gregory a smoothie, a smile spreading across his face. "Thanks, man, I really appreciate your support."

As they sipped their drinks, Jack couldn't help but daydream about his future with Amelia. He was excited for the possibility of finally having someone special in his life, and he knew that with a little bravery and persistence, anything was possible.

"What are you doing for Christmas, Jack?" asked Gregory.

"I'm going to spend some time with my family. We're going to have a big dinner and exchange gifts," replied Jack. "And well, some annoying extended family members are coming."

"That must suck," Gregory said. Jack let out an exasperated sigh. "It does." He went to serve some tables the cream pies they ordered.

"So, I heard that the bake shop is closing down for a few days," Gregory said.

"Yes, it is. We all need a break, and the owner wants to spend some time with his family too," replied Jack.

"That's great. I think it's important to take a break and recharge."

"I agree. And I think it's a good opportunity for us to reflect on our lives and think about what we want to achieve in the coming year," Jack added.

"Definitely. Maybe I will finally be able to get a car next year," Gregory said, his eyes lighting up with excitement.

"That's great, Gregory. I think you'll be amazing at it," said Jack, smiling.

The two friends talked for a while longer, discussing their plans and aspirations for the future.

As Greg finished his drink and said goodbye, they bid each other goodbye. Jack felt uplifted and inspired by his conversation with Gregory. He was grateful for their friendship and the support they provided each other.

Jack couldn't wait to see Amelia. He stood at the entrance of the park; his heart was pounding with excitement. He had no idea what Amelia had in store for him, but he was sure it would be a surprise he would never forget.

He made his way through the park, taking in the sights and sounds of the lush green trees, the chirping of the birds, and the laughter of children playing. He felt at peace here, surrounded by nature and away from the noise and chaos of the city. He made his way to the agreed-upon spot where he was to meet Amelia, a small area under a big oak tree.

As he approached, he saw Amelia sitting there, her long dark hair flowing in the light breeze. She was wearing a bright yellow jacket that made her look like a ray of sunshine on an otherwise dreary day. Jack's heart skipped a beat as he gazed at her, and he felt a wave of love wash over him.

"Amelia," he called out, she flinched and looked up at him.

"Oh, Jack," she responded. She got on her feet and dusted her jeans as she walked towards him.

They both felt a surge of happiness at being reunited after what felt like an eternity, even though neither was exactly willing to admit it.

Amelia initiated a hug which was very short-lived and slightly awkward, but Jack didn't mind.

They pulled away from each other, still smiling, and Amelia took Jack's hand.

"I want to show you something," she said, leading him towards the woods. "What?" He asked with curiosity laced in his voice.

"You'll see," she squealed as she dragged him further away from the boundaries of the park.

Amelia led him deeper into the woods. The sound of chirping birds and rustling leaves filled the air as they jogged deeper into the woods. The adrenal rush Amelia felt as she pulled Jack toward her favorite spot was almost refreshing.

"This is my favorite spot," Amelia said, as they approached a small clearing. "I come here whenever I need to escape the world and just be at peace."

Jack looked around, taking in the beauty of the place. A small stream flowed through the clearing, surrounded by wildflowers and tall trees. The sun shone down, dappling the ground with light.

"It's amazing," Jack said, genuinely impressed.

"I'm glad you like it," Amelia replied, a smile spreading across her face. "I used to come here as a child with my parents. We would picnic and play in the stream. It's a special place for me."

She led Jack over to a large rock by the stream and sat down. Jack sat next to her, the water gurgling softly beside them.

"I can see why this is your favorite spot," Jack said. "It's so peaceful and calm here."

"Exactly," Amelia said. "I come here to think, to relax, and to just be. It's a reminder that life doesn't always have to be so fast-paced and hectic."

They sat in silence for a few moments, taking in the beauty of the place. A butterfly flitted by, landing on a nearby flower.

"This is the kind of place where you can forget all your troubles," Jack said.

"Yes," Amelia agreed. "It's a place where I feel connected to nature, to the world around me. It's a reminder that we're all part of something bigger than ourselves."

She turned to Jack and took his hand.

"I wanted to bring you here because I care about you," she said, her voice soft. "I wanted you to experience this place, to see why it's so special to me. And I wanted to share it with you."

Jack looked at her, his eyes filled with love.

"Amelia, I'm so grateful that you brought me here," he said. "This is a truly special place, and I'm honored that you wanted to share it with me. I'll never forget this moment."

They sat there for a while longer, taking in the peace and quiet of the woods, surrounded by the beauty of nature. Jack had been looking forward to this moment all day. He had something very important to tell Amelia, and he was hoping she would feel the same way.

As they sat on a fallen log, Jack took a deep breath and turned to Amelia. She looked at him with a smile, her eyes shining in the sun. "What's up, Jack?" she asked.

"Amelia," he started, his voice slightly shaky. "I've been meaning to tell you something for a while now. And I couldn't think of a better place to say it than here, surrounded by all this beauty."

Amelia's smile faded, and she looked at him with a hint of concern. "Is everything okay?" she asked.

"Yes, everything is more than okay," Jack said, taking her hand. "Amelia, you know I love you. But it is more than that you are also my everything."

Amelia's eyes widened in surprise, and she looked at Jack for a long moment, as if trying to understand what he had just said. "Jack," she finally said, her voice barely above a whisper, "I… I don't know what to say I-"

"I know," Jack said, feeling a little deflated. "It's all happening too fast, I caught you unaware, I understand, but I can't deny my feelings anymore. I love you, Amelia. I love the way you laugh and the way you look at the world. I love everything about you, and I just want to be with you."

Amelia was silent for a moment, and Jack held his breath, waiting for her response. Finally, she looked up at him, her eyes shining with tears. "Jack," she said, her voice choking with emotion. "I love you too."

Jack's heart skipped a beat, and he felt like he was on top of the world. He pulled Amelia into a tight embrace, kissing her hair and holding her close. "I promise I'll always be here for you," he whispered. "I'll always love you, no matter what."

They stayed like that for a long time, just holding each other and feeling the love that had been there all along. Finally, they pulled back and looked into each other's eyes, smiling, and laughing through their tears.

"I can't believe this is happening," Amelia said, her voice still choked with emotion. "I fell in love with someone I just met a week ago."

"Me neither," Jack said, smiling. "But I'm so glad it did. I'm so grateful to have you in my life, Amelia."

They sat together in the clearing, talking and laughing and just enjoying each other's company. The sun was setting, casting a warm glow over the forest, and Jack and Amelia knew that their lives would never be the same. They had found love in the most unexpected place, and they were never going to let it go.

They made their way back to the trailhead, hand in hand. Jack spared a second look at the clearing they had just left and smiled.

Chapter Eight

Mr. Muller sat on his front porch, staring out into the distance. He was mourning the loss of his wife, who was a victim of the mysterious disappearances. Despite the passage of time, he still felt the same overwhelming sadness that had gripped him on the day she was declared missing.

The once vibrant and bustling neighborhood had fallen silent, reflecting the emptiness that now filled Mr. Muller's heart. He remembered the times when his wife would sit beside him on the porch, holding his hand and chatting about the events of the day. Now, he was alone, and the memories of their life together only served to amplify his grief.

He tried to find comfort in the memories, but they only brought him more pain. He thought of the laughter they had shared, the trips they had taken, and the future they had once dreamed of. Now, those dreams were gone, along with his wife.

He gazed out at the yard, where his wife had spent so many hours tending to her garden. He remembered how she had loved the smell of freshly cut flowers and the feel of the soil on her hands. He tried to picture her smile, but the image was fading, as though his memory of her was slowly slipping away.

Mr. Muller felt a fresh wave of desperation wash over him. He was afraid that he would forget her, that the love they had shared would fade away into the emptiness of time. He longed for her touch, for her voice, for her presence in his life. He wanted to hold her once again, but he knew that was impossible.

Tears filled his eyes, and he wept silently, overwhelmed by the weight of his loss. He realized that his life would never be the same, that the void left by his wife's passing would never be filled. He was alone now, and he felt that he would never find happiness again.

He sat on the porch for hours, lost in thought and memories. As the sun began to set, he finally got up and went inside, feeling exhausted and drained. He went to bed, but he didn't sleep. Instead, he lay in the dark, listening to the sound of his own breathing and feeling the weight of his loss.

The next day, he rose early and went back out to the porch. He sat there, staring out at the world, and he knew that he would never fully recover from the loss of his wife. He would always feel the emptiness, the sadness, and the longing. But he also knew that he would always carry her memory with him and that the love they had shared would live on, even if she was no longer there.

Jack sat on his couch, scrolling through his phone in anticipation, he was waiting to receive a reply from Amelia. Tim walked past him. "Hey Tim, where are you going?"

Tim frowned, "Grandma wants a foot massage and Mom said I should do it," he said with a pout. "Yeesh, you're on your own little bud," he said as he threw his arms into the air in surrender. He slouched his back against the chair and continued to scroll through his phone.

His aunt and mother had gone out together on a spa date while Steve and Victor went to play golf, leaving just the kids at home.

One of his cousins, Billy, burst in.

"Jack, my man! What's up?" Billy said, with a huge grin on his face.

Jack sighed. "Hey, Billy. I'm just trying to relax. What do you want?"

"Relax? It's the weekend, man! Let's go party!"

"I don't want to party, Billy. I just want to stay in and relax," Jack replied, trying to keep the annoyance out of his voice.

Billy rolled his eyes. "Come on, Jack. When was the last time you had any fun?"

"I have fun," Jack said defensively. "I just have a different definition of fun than you do."

"Well, your definition of fun is boring. Let's go out and live a little," Billy said, grabbing Jack's arm and pulling him up from the couch.

Jack reluctantly followed Billy out of the apartment and into the night.

Jack walked into the club, the thumping bass of the music already giving him a headache. He hated clubs, the loud music, the flashing lights, and the crowds of people made him feel suffocated.

Billy, who was grinning from ear to ear blended perfectly into the club scenery. "C'mon go there!" He said, making sure to amplify his voice as he pointed towards the direction. Jack sighed and followed his lead, dodging dancing bodies and spilled drinks.

Billy quickly began mingling and mixing with people in the club, while Jack watched with his ever-growing annoyance. Billy had always been overbearing, and his persistent personality made it difficult to resist him. Once again, just like he had many times in the past, Billy had put Jack in a position he didn't want to be in.

Billy walked up to him with two shots of eggnog, one in each arm. "Hey! Are you having fun?!"

"Yeah, barely," Jack replied, trying to hide the annoyance in his voice. "Why did you make me come here again?"

"Come on, Jack! Live a little! You're always cooped up at home, you need to let loose and have some fun," Billy replied, his eyes shining with excitement as he shoved the drink towards Jack's face.

Jack rolled his eyes and took a sip of his drink, the bitter taste trailed down his throat, doing nothing to improve his mood. He leaned against the bar and watched as Billy danced with a group of girls, his cousin's laughter ringing out above the music.

He wished he could be more like Billy, carefree and able to have a good time no matter where he was. But the club just wasn't for him, and he longed for the peace and quiet of his own home.

As the night wore on, Jack's patience wore thin. He decided he had had enough and was about to leave when Billy grabbed him by the arm.

"Come on, one more drink for the road?" Billy pleaded, signaling for the bartender.

"I've had enough, Billy. I'm going home," Jack replied, pulling his arm away.

"Come on, one more drink for the road?" Billy pleaded, signaling for the bartender.

"I've had enough, Billy. I'm going home," Jack replied, pulling his arm away.

"Fine, be a party pooper," Billy said, shrugging.

Jack nodded and made his way out of the club, the cool night air a welcome relief from the hot and noisy club. He took a deep breath and smiled, glad to be away from the club and back to his quiet and peaceful life.

Finally, after what felt like hours, they made it back home. As they kicked off their shoes and made their way to the couch, Jack announced that he wanted to watch an action movie. Billy, on the other hand, was in the mood for a romantic comedy. The two of them argued back and forth for a few minutes, each trying to convince the other to watch their preferred genre.

"Boys, are you okay?" Jack's mom asked concern etched on her face as she descended the stairs.

"We're fine, Mom," Jack said dismissively.

"Let's watch a movie and unwind before bed," Billy suggested, breaking the silence.

Everyone seemed to agree. "What are you two arguing about?" Miranda asked.

"Action movie or romantic comedy," Billy said, shrugging.

"Oh, romantic comedy all the way," Lisa said, smiling.

"Definitely a romantic comedy," Miranda added, much to Jack's surprise.

"You know what, Billy? I'm done," Jack said, his annoyance finally boiling over. "I'm tired of you always trying to drag me out and do things I don't want to do. I'm just not in the mood for it tonight." The frustration was evident in his voice.

"What's your problem?" Billy asked, sitting up and giving Jack a confused look.

"You're my problem, Billy. You always have to be the center of attention and do everything as loudly as possible. I just can't handle it anymore," Jack said, letting out a long sigh.

He turned around and headed to his room. He slammed his door shut and plopped on his bed, staring at his ceiling. He closed his eyes and inhaled sharply, enjoying the peacefulness of his room.

He reached for his phone and swiped it open, his heart pounding in his chest as he tried to gather the courage to hit the send button on the message he had just typed.

His fingers hovered over the keys as he thought about what to say. He wanted to be witty and charming, but he didn't want to come across as desperate. Finally, he settled on a simple message: "Hey, Amelia. Just wanted to say I had a great time talking to you today. How's your day going?"

He hit the send button and took a deep breath. The waiting was the hardest part. He drummed his fingers on the table, trying to distract himself. Suddenly, his phone vibrated. He grabbed it, eager to see Amelia's response.

"Hey, Jack! My day's going pretty well, thanks for asking. What have you been up to?"

Jack smiled, relieved that she was responding. He quickly typed out a reply.

"Just hanging out at home. Trying to catch up on some reading. How about you? What have you been up to?"

"Oh, just running some errands and hanging out with friends. Nothing too exciting," Amelia replied.

Jack could feel the conversation flowing naturally. They talked about everything from their favorite books to their favorite TV shows. He felt like he could talk to her for hours.

"Jack, I really appreciate you telling me how you feel. To be honest, I've had feelings for you too. I was just too scared to say anything. But now that you've said it, I'm so glad we can talk about it."

Jack felt a wave of relief wash over him. He smiled so widely that his cheeks hurt. They continued talking for a while longer until Amelia had to go. They made plans to meet up soon and get to know each other better.

As Jack put his phone down, he realized that he was grinning from ear to ear. He couldn't believe that the girl he liked felt the same way. He felt like he was walking on air. He couldn't wait to see where this would lead.

Gregory walked nervously into the police station, clutching his ID and freshly-printed résumé. He had always dreamed of becoming a police officer and working for the betterment of society, and now, finally, he had the opportunity to turn his dream into a reality as a new intern at the station. He was eager to learn, work hard, and make a positive impact on his community.

As he entered the main lobby, he was greeted by a friendly face. "Hi, you must be

Gregory! I'm Officer Jenkins. Welcome to the station," said the officer, extending his hand. Gregory shook it eagerly and introduced himself.

"I'm so excited to be here," he said, beaming with pride. "I've always wanted to work in law enforcement and make a difference in people's lives."

"That's great to hear," Officer Jenkins said with a smile. "Follow me, I'll show you around and introduce you to everyone."

The station was buzzing with activity as Gregory followed Officer Jenkins through the hallways. They stopped at several different offices, where Gregory met detectives, officers, and other staff members. They were all friendly and welcoming, and Gregory felt like he was already part of the team.

As they walked, Officer Jenkins explained some of the station's processes and procedures to Gregory. "It's important that you understand how everything works here," he said. "We all work together to keep the community safe and solve crimes, and it's important that everyone is on the same page."

Gregory listened attentively, taking in all the information he could. He was fascinated by the work that the police officers did, and he was eager to be a part of it. Especially now that he would officially be the contact point between the neighborhood watch he formed and the police department.

Eventually, they reached the break room, where Gregory met his supervisor, Chief Ramirez. "Gregory, this is Chief Ramirez. He'll be overseeing your internship and making sure you get the most out of your experience here."

Gregory introduced himself to the chief and they discussed his goals and expectations for the internship. Chief Ramirez was impressed by Gregory's enthusiasm and passion for law enforcement, and he agreed to provide him with the best possible training and experience.

Gregory was to spend most of his time observing and learning from the officers on the job. He would shadow detectives as they conducted investigations, and he would assist officers with paperwork and other tasks. He was also obligated to attend meetings and briefings, where he would learn about new developments in the community and how the police were working to address them.

The day was generally slow-paced and boring, there wasn't much to do and because he lacked experience, Jenkins decided it was best to have him do more administrative work in the meantime. It was now lunch break and Gregory was at the cafeteria with some other colleagues, they were having some donuts and sodas.

Marai strode into the police department's cafeteria, her duty belt jingling softly with each step. She was a tall, imposing figure with piercing blue eyes and hair pulled back in a severe bun. As she scanned the room, her gaze settled on Gregory, an intern who had just started his first week on the job.

She approached the plus-sized young man with tousled brown hair and a smattering of freckles across his nose. He was hunched over a plate of donuts, his attention focused solely on the sugary treats in front of him.

"You got some jam over there," a feminine voice rang, Gregory raised his head to face her. His eyes widened in surprise at the sight of Marai. He quickly wiped his mouth with a napkin and cleared his throat, brushing crumbs from his shirt. "Oh, hi, Marai," he said, sounding flustered.

"What are you doing?" She asked in a stern no-nonsense voice.

"I was just having a snack. Is something wrong?"

Marai raised an eyebrow. "Do you think it's appropriate to be eating donuts on the job, Gregory?" she asked.

Gregory blinked. "I, uh, it's my lunch break," he said.

Marai sighed and shook her head, "that lunch break expired one minute ago," she tried with folded arms. He mouthed an "oh" with his lips.

"And plus, as a police officer, you need to be aware of your image and the message it sends to the public," she said. "Eating junk food in uniform can give people the wrong impression. You need to be setting a positive example, not indulging in unhealthy habits."

Gregory nodded, looking chagrined. "I'm sorry, Marai. I didn't realize," he said.

Marai softened her tone, sensing that the young man was genuinely remorseful. "It's okay, Gregory," she said. "Just try to make better choices in the future. Now, I need to talk to you about your role here at the department."

Gregory looked up, his eyes brightening with interest. "Sure, what do you need from me?" he asked.

Marai sat down across from him and leaned forward, her elbows resting on the table. "As you know, you're an intern here, and I'm in charge of overseeing your training and development," she said. "I expect a lot from my team, and I want to make sure you have the tools and skills you need to succeed."

Gregory nodded eagerly. "I'm ready to learn, Marai," he said. "I want to be the best cop I can be."

Marai smiled, pleased by the young man's attitude. "Good, I'm glad to hear that," she said. "Now, let's go over some of the basics. First of all, always be professional, both in your behavior and in your appearance. Always be on time and ready to go when it's time to hit the streets."

Gregory nodded, taking notes in a small notebook. "Got it, always be professional and on time," he said.

Marai continued, "Next, always be aware of your surroundings and pay attention to detail. The little things can sometimes be the most important. And finally, always be respectful to your fellow officers, the people you serve, and to yourself."

Gregory nodded again, looking serious. "I understand, Marai," he said. "I won't let you down."

Marai smiled. "I know you won't, Gregory," she said. "You have a lot of potential, and I'm here to help you reach it. Now, let's get to work."

With that, Marai stood up, motioning for him to follow her. As their conversation continued down the hallway, Gregory couldn't help but feel grateful for this chance encounter. He had never been one to make friends easily, but something about Marai just clicked.

As Gregory headed back to the police station, he felt a sense of excitement and happiness that he hadn't felt in a long time.

Sussie arrived at Jack's house in the morning to help his mother and aunt Lisa bake brownies. Though she was excited to spend some time with them and help out in the kitchen, she had an ulterior motive for coming, she wanted to spend some time with Jack.

Throughout the morning, Jack seemed distant and uninterested in speaking to Sussie. He would quickly leave the room whenever she entered and refused to make eye contact. Sussie was confused and hurt by Jack's behavior. She had always considered him a close friend and was unsure of what she had done wrong.

Miranda and Lisa were talking about some egg discounts at the supermarket when Suisse took the opportunity to slip out of the kitchen and look for him.

Sussie nervously knocked on the door of Jack's room, her heart racing with excitement. She had been crushing on Jack for months, and she had finally mustered up the courage to talk to him. As she waited for him to answer the door, she practiced what she wanted to say over and over in her head.

Finally, the door creaked open, and Jack appeared. He was tall and lean, with piercing blue eyes and a warm smile that lit up his face. Sussie felt her knees go weak, but she forced herself to stand tall and smile back at him.

"Hey Jack," she called with a small smile on her face. He held back the urge to groan and just harrumphed instead. "What do you want?" His muffled voice rang. "Nothing I just wanted to drop by," she said as she entered the room and closed the doors behind her. She gently walked towards his bed and sat by the edge, observing him with eyes full of admiration.

"I was just passing by and I thought I'd pop in and say hello," Sussie said, trying to sound casual.

"Cool," Jack said in a stoic tone, "What brings you here?" He added.

Sussie's heart was pounding as she sat in Jack's room. It was a mess, with clothes and books scattered everywhere, but to her, it was the most perfect room in the world. She took a deep breath and turned to face Jack.

"I was just wondering if we could talk for a bit?" Sussie asked, looking up at him with hopeful eyes.

"Sure," Jack said as he took a seat beside her in his bed. "What's on your mind?"

Sussie sat down on the edge of the bed and took a deep breath. "I just wanted to say that I've had a crush on you for a long time now, and I was hoping that maybe we could go out on a date or something?"

Jack's eyes widened in surprise, and he looked at Sussie for a long moment. "Really? I had no idea," he said finally. "I mean, I think you're great, Sussie, but I don't know if I'm ready for a relationship right now. I'm sorry," he lied, that was his excuse to get her off his back.

Sussie felt her heart sink. She had been so sure that Jack was into her, and now she felt foolish for thinking that he would feel the same way. She stood up from the bed, feeling embarrassed.

"It's okay," she said, trying to hide the disappointment in her voice. "I understand. I'll see you around, Jack."

"Sure, thing Sue."

Sussie turned to face him, her eyes filled with tears. "I really like you, Jack. I don't want to push you into anything you're not ready for, but I just had to tell you how I feel."

Jack looked at her, and Sussie could see the confusion in his eyes. He took a deep breath and sighed. "you're just a friend Sussie, sorry." She felt a fresh wave of despair wash over her. "Of course, Jack. I'm just glad we had this talk. I'll see you around," she replied as she swallowed the bile that was forming in her throat.

With a fake smile, she turned and walked out of Jack's room, feeling worse than she had in a long time. She knew that she had taken a risk by telling Jack how she felt, but it was a risk that had paid off.

Just then, his phone buzzed and he checked it. It was a text from Amelia.

Let's meet at our spot, later this evening - at 12:24 pm.

He locked his phone screen with a wide smile.

Sussie hastily descended the stairs, allowing her fingers to glide over the rails as she did. "Oh, honey Miranda was just looking for you-"

"I'm not feeling too well," she said, interjecting Lisa mid-speech. "I think I need to go home." Just as Lisa was about to respond Miranda came out of the kitchen with a spatula within her grip. "What's going on?" She asked, sensing the uneasiness. Sussie sniffed, trying her best to hold back tears. "I'm sorry, I just need to go home. I'm not feeling well."

Miranda's eyes widened, "oh sorry please go ahead dear." Sussie mouthed a small thank you, her voice clouded in emotions and her eyes teary. She rushed to the door and banged it shut behind her as she jogged towards her house. Lisa and Miranda shared a look, "what was that about?" Lisa asked. Miranda looked at the staircase, her eyes trailing them up to Jack's bedroom. "I'll be back."

She stormed off towards Jack's room, leaving behind a confused Lisa. Miranda burst into Jack's room, her eyes blazing with anger. Jack was sprawled on his bed, about to start playing a video game, when she stormed in.

"Jack! What have you done?" Miranda cried.

Jack looked up, taken aback by his mother's sudden appearance. "What are you talking about?" he asked, sounding defensive.

"You know exactly what I'm talking about," Miranda said, her voice rising. He groaned when he realized.

"It was just a stupid crush," Jack said dismissively. "She'll get over it."

"Get over it?" Miranda repeated, incredulous. "Do you have any idea how much it hurts to have your heart broken? And you just casually dismissed it as a stupid crush. That's not how you treat people, Jack."

"I didn't mean to hurt her, but I don't like her," Jack said.

"That doesn't change the fact that you did hurt her," Miranda said sternly. "Your actions have consequences, and you need to be more considerate of other people's feelings."

"It's not my fault. I already told her sorry."

"Sorry isn't enough," Miranda said. "You need to take responsibility for what you've done and make it right. You need to apologize to Sussie and show her that you're truly sorry for what you've done."

Jack sighed. "Apologize for what? Not liking her?"

"Jack!"

"What Mom?"

She shook her head slowly, "You better make it up to her at the Christmas Eve party."

"I'm not going," he mumbled. "Oh yes you will," she said in a low tone that resembled a threat. He sighed and dropped on his bed.

Mr. Muller was on his porch as usual, the chilly winter breeze did nothing to deter him from staying outside. He had a cup of hot cocoa in his arms as he rocked back and forth on his chair. He thought about the mysterious disappearances in Candland and wondered what the cause could be.

Muller came to the resolve that maybe it was time to leave Candland and its sour memories behind. He sighed deeply and began to think of where he could stay.

It was blank.

He tried to recollect any other geographical locations he could live in but there was nothing. He realized he had lived in Candland all his life. He looked at his arms with scrutiny. He noticed that he, along with everyone else in the town, were merely gingerbread cookies. He was shocked and confused, unable to understand how this could be possible. He had never questioned the reality of his existence before, but now he couldn't ignore the truth that was staring him in the face. He wondered if there was anything beyond Candland, he began to ponder deeply on his origins, the people of Candland all seemed to spawn into existence. His neighbor's daughter Martha was never here some months ago, someday she was just around and nobody questioned it. He rushed inside his house and began tearing it apart. His doorknobs were made of icing and the stairs were merely chocolate bars. He was horrified by this awakening.

He wandered the streets of the gingerbread town, talking to the other gingerbreads about what he had discovered. Some of them were dismissive of his claims, while others were horrified at the thought that they were not real beings. As he spoke with the others, Mr. Muller began to realize that they were all just gingerbreads like any other pastry and that their lives were controlled by the whims of the person who created them.

The reality of the situation was overwhelming for Mr. Muller. He had lost his wife, and now he was facing the fact that his entire life had been a fabrication. He felt as if he was trapped in a never-ending nightmare, with no way to escape.

He struggled to come to terms with his newfound understanding of the world. He felt disconnected from the other gingerbreads as if he was the only one who truly understood the truth.

Jack wore a pair of jeans with a white shirt as he prepared to go out. Billy stuck his head into his room. "Where are you going?" He asked in an inquisitive tone. "None of your business Billy," he spat back and bent lower as he slapped some gel against his hair. He took one last look in the mirror, took a deep breath, and headed out the door, walking past Billy. As he jogged down the stairs he saw Tim and Isabella arguing about something but paid them no heed. "Jack where are you going!?" Miranda asked from the dining area. "I'm going to see someone; I'll be back by 7!" He yelled back before exiting.

The woods were about a half-hour walk from Jack's house. The sun was shining, birds were chirping, and a light breeze was blowing through the trees, making the walk enjoyable. As Jack approached the meeting spot, his heart started to race. He could see Amelia waiting for him, leaning against a tree, looking as beautiful as ever in a black skirt and a pair of heeled boots. Her jacket wrapped around her just perfectly and the ⅔ sleeves were appropriately styled.

"Hi, Jack!" Amelia greeted him with a warm smile.

"Hi, Amelia," Jack replied, smiling back. "You look amazing."

"Thank you," Amelia blushed.

Jack could feel his nerves starting to ease as they chatted and got to know each other better.

"Wait, I brought something."

She opened her bag and brought out a pack. "I made some pancakes; would you like to try them?" Jack chuckled, "of course."

She reached into her bag and brought out a flat plate. She shared the pancakes into two equal portions. Jack poured the sugar syrup over the pancakes and began shoving them into his mouth, he chewed ecstatically, allowing the rich milky flavor to dissolve in his mouth. He groaned in appreciation and his eyes rolled to the back of his head. "It's so good, you have to tell me the recipe," he complimented.

Her lips twitched into a smile, "I made it with love," she said and looked into his eyes. He smiled back at her and whispered in a husky voice, "Thank you."

They talked about everything, from their interests and hobbies to their hopes and dreams for the future. Jack was amazed at how easy it was to talk to Amelia, and he felt like he had known her for years.

As the sun started to set, Jack and Amelia took a walk around the clearing, admiring the beauty of the woods as the light changed. They talked about their future plans and what they wanted to do together. They walked slowly away from their spot; Jack was thinking about how to ask Amelia to be his girlfriend. He looked over his shoulders at her, "Amelia," he started, she paused and looked at him with an inquisitive gaze, as if to say, 'Go on.'

"I haven't asked you out formally, and I know this might not be the best place but... will you be my girlfriend?"

Amelia's eyes widened in excitement, "yes, yes Jack I will!" She squealed as she jumped to hug him. She wrapped her legs around his torso and hung her arms around the base of his neck, he reciprocated the hug and spun her around as a wave of joy washed over him. Cheerful chuckles escaped from her as he carried her weight. Eventually, Jack tripped and fell flat on his back, she landed on top of him and her hair fell against her back as she faced him. An awkward silence lingered between the two for a few seconds before Amelia connected her lips with his, eliminating the space between the two of them.

She rotated her head as she continued her lustful invasion of his mouth, Jack snaked his arms around her waist to hold her in place as they intensified their kiss. They broke apart and she got on her feet first with a smile plastered on her lips. Jack bit his lower lip slowly and licked it with his tongue, "just like candy," he whispered as he looked at her with a mischievous smile. Amelia playfully swatted his arm, "let's go silly," she said as she let a small snicker escape from her mouth.

When Amelia got home she opened her front door and dashed inside the house, then twisted around to close the door. By the time she turned to face her front, Rodolfo was already in the scope of her vision and it slightly startled her. "Dad.." she trailed off as she looked at the impassive expression spread across his features. "Where have you been Amelia?" She swallowed, "I just went to see some friends." With that reply, she was ready to escape to her room but Rodolfo wasn't having it. "What friends? What are their names?" He asked, freezing her in her tracks.

She stayed silent as she tried to fabricate the most believable lie within seconds, the gears in her mind grinding and turning. "Stacey and Emma."

"Where do you know them from?"

"Dad I'm an adult I can go out if-"

"Don't use that tone on me, young lady!" He yelled as he pointed intensely towards her. Sarah's room door clicked open and she walked out, "Don't transfer your aggression on my daughter!" She defended. Amelia's tongue was caught in her mouth as she witnessed the sudden outbursts from her mother. "You say it like she's not my daughter as well, if she's hanging out with bad company I deserve to know!"

"Oh please, since when did Amelia going out become such a problem? Rodolfo, stop picking on Amelia."

"Picking on her? Sarah, can you hear yourself!?"

Amelia inched towards the stairs as their argument continued to escalate, they were both so engrossed with their screaming match that they didn't notice when Amelia went up the stairs and into her room, locking the doors behind her as she cried on her bed.

Chapter Nine

Christmas Eve was in two days, Miranda had gone over the top to ensure that everyone had gotten a befitting outfit since the theme for the day was old school. Jack was generally very uninterested and it got on her nerves, nonetheless, she got him a cowboy outfit.

Sussie's father and Victor had agreed to play chess at Sussie's place and much to Jack's dismay Miranda made sure that the rest of the family offered help in one way or the other in planning the party which meant they would be going to her house. Billy had tagged along under the guise that he wanted to help but the truth was that he developed a slight crush on Sussie and hoped to be able to get to know her more.

Miranda pressed the button for the doorbell and they all waited in anticipation. Soon the door clicked open and Sussie appeared behind it. She greeted them with a small wave and maintained a neutral facial expression when she faced Jack. He was happy that she had finally moved on, at least that's what he thought.

She moved out of the way and let them in, Jack entered last and didn't acknowledge Sussie as he did.

The hallway of the no-house was spacious and well-lit, with large windows that let in plenty of natural light. The walls were painted a warm cream color, and the floor was covered in a plush beige carpet. A large wooden console table stood against one wall, displaying a vase of freshly-cut flowers and a decorative mirror.

At the end of the hallway was a set of double doors that led into the sitting room. The room was cozy and inviting, with plush sofas and armchairs arranged around a stone fireplace. The fireplace was the centerpiece of the room, with a flickering fire that cast a warm glow over the room. Above the fireplace hung a large oil painting, depicting a peaceful countryside scene.

In one corner of the room was a grand piano, its glossy black surface reflecting the light from the chandelier above. The chandelier was a beautiful piece, made of sparkling crystal, and it cast a warm glow over the room. The furniture was upholstered in a rich burgundy fabric, adding to the room's warm and inviting feel.

Overall, the interior of Sussie's house was a testament to her family's wealth and good taste. It was a warm and welcoming space that invited guests to sit and relax in comfort.

It was obvious to Jack that Sussie's family was at least moderately rich.

Gregory sat at his desk, surrounded by piles of paperwork. As a police intern, he was tasked with sorting through evidence for an ongoing investigation. It was his second day on the job, and he was eager to prove himself to his boss, Marai.

Marai was a seasoned detective, known for her strict attention to detail and no-nonsense approach to police work. Gregory was intimidated by her reputation but also inspired by her dedication to justice. He was determined to live up to her expectations and make a positive impact on the police force.

As he sifted through the stack of evidence, Gregory tried to focus on his task. He had to make sure that each piece of evidence was properly labeled and stored in the right place. It was a tedious process, but he was determined to do it right.

Just as he was getting into the rhythm of his work, Marai walked over to his desk. Gregory sat up straight, trying to appear as professional as possible.

"How's it going, Gregory?" Marai asked, her eyes scanning the piles of paperwork on his desk.

"It's going well, thank you," Gregory replied. "I'm trying to get through this stack of evidence as quickly as I can."

Marai nodded, a small smile playing at the corners of her mouth. "Good work. I know it's not the most exciting part of police work, but it's crucial for making sure that justice is served."

Gregory nodded eagerly. "I understand, and I'm happy to do whatever I can to help."

Marai gave him a firm pat on the back. "I appreciate that attitude, Gregory. Keep up the good work."

With that, Marai turned and walked away, leaving Gregory to continue his task. He felt a surge of pride and determination. He was determined to show Marai that he was a valuable member of the team.

For the next few hours, Gregory worked steadily, sorting through the evidence, and making sure that everything was properly labeled and stored. As he worked, he couldn't help but think about the cases that the evidence was related to. He wondered about the people involved and what had led them to this point. And his apprehensiveness grew as more cases of mysterious disappearances kept coming.

He also thought about Marai and the other detectives on the force. They were the ones who were out there on the front lines, gathering evidence and making arrests. Gregory was grateful for the opportunity to work alongside them and learn from their experiences.

Just as he was finishing up the last of the evidence, Marai walked back over to his desk. Gregory sat up straight, ready to hear what she had to say.

"How's it going, Gregory?" Marai asked, her eyes once again scanning the piles of paperwork.

"It's going well, thank you," Gregory replied, feeling a sense of pride at how organized his desk had become.

Marai nodded, a look of satisfaction on her face. "I can see that you've been working hard. You have a good eye for detail, and that's exactly what we need in this department."

Gregory felt his chest swell with pride. "Thank you, Marai. I'm just happy to be able to help in any way I can."

Marai gave him a firm pat on the back. "I have a feeling that you're going to make a great detective someday, Gregory. Keep up the good work."

With that, Marai turned and walked away, leaving Gregory feeling inspired and motivated. For her, it was a busy day at the police station, she and the other officers were rushing back and forth, trying to handle the numerous calls coming in.

Chief Ramirez was in his office, deep in thought, staring at the map of the city on his wall. A new wave of disappearances had hit the city and it seemed to be spreading fast, with no pattern in sight.

Just then, Marai, one of the veteran officers, entered the room, looking just as troubled as the Chief. "We're short on men, Chief," she said, "I need to go out there and investigate, but I can't go alone."

Chief Thomas nodded, understanding the

gravity of the situation. "Take Gregory with you," he said, pointing to the new intern who was sitting at his desk, looking bewildered. "He's the only one available right now."

Marai scoffed in disbelief, "he's only been working here for two days chief, I think I'd be better off waiting for Jenkins." "There's an emergency, we can't wait, besides it's not a dangerous mission, it's just an investigation, take the lad."

She sighed and made her way over to Gregory. "Come on, let's go," she said, trying to sound as reassuring as possible. "Go where?" he asked, confused by her statement, he knew he wasn't due for any kind of fieldwork for the next few weeks. "To a crime scene." She put her hands in her back pocket and began walking towards the door.

Gregory gathered his things and followed her out to the police car.

As they drove through the city, Marai filled Gregory in on the details of the case. "These kidnappings are random and seem to be happening all over the city. We need to find out if there's a pattern and stop it before it gets any worse."

Gregory nodded, taking in the information. "I understand," he said, "but what can I do to help?"

Marai gave him a sidelong glance. "Just stick with me and observe, for now. We'll see what you can do once we get there."

They arrived at the scene of the latest kidnapping, a small apartment complex on the outskirts of the town. The residents were all gathered outside, looking scared and confused. Marai and Gregory made their way through the crowd and approached the building's manager. "What happened here?" Marai asked.

The manager's hands were shaking as he spoke. "One of the tenants, Mrs. Johnson, was taken from her apartment's balcony early this morning. We haven't seen or heard from her since."

Marai took out her notebook and jotted down the information. "Do you have a description of the kidnapper?" she asked.

The manager shook his head. "No, nobody saw anything. It all happened so fast; she was just... gone!"

Marai sighed, frustrated. "Alright, we'll start canvassing the area and see if anyone saw anything." She turned to Gregory. "Come on, let's go."

They spent the next several hours talking to the residents and searching for any clues. The kidnappings had everyone on edge and it seemed like nobody had seen or heard anything useful. Marai was about to give up when Gregory suddenly spoke up. "Wait a minute," he said, "I think I found something."

Marai looked up from her notes and followed his gaze to a nearby dumpster. "What is it?" she asked.

Gregory pointed at a portion of the trail that looked like it was scratched off. Marai walked over and lowered herself to the ground, careful not to touch it. "Good work," she said, examining the mark. "These look like something big, something sharp destroying the floor. We might be dealing with something much more sophisticated than we thought." Gregory's eyes lit up with excitement. "That means we might have a lead!"

Marai nodded, looking more determined than ever. "Let's go back to the station and see if we can track down whoever is behind this," she said as she put a call out to alert the forensic team.

Jack climbed the ladder and helped to hang up the strips of Christmas lights while Sussie was outside with Tim and Isabella. When he was done, he dipped his hand into his pocket to retrieve his phone while still on the top of the ladder. He checked if Amelia had replied to his text message where he asked if they would meet up at that spot later in the evening.

See you by 6 - 3:46 pm

He smiled at his phone and shoved it back into his pocket. "Boo!" His cousin's voice caught him by surprise causing him to flinch and let go of the ladder, he fell to the ground, landing first on his thigh. "Ouch!' he yelled, sprawling on the floor in pain.

"Ouu sorry man," Billy said, chuckling. Jack rolled his eyes as he got on his feet and dusted the back of his trousers.

"So cuz, how's it going?"

"Just great, Billy. I love decorating for parties I don't even want to attend and falling from ladders," he said, giving his cousin a death stare.

"Ah come on, it'll be fun. Plus, think of all the cute girls that'll be here tonight."

Jack rolled his eyes and continued hanging the smaller decorations. "Hey, my leg hurts so you hang the mistletoe," he ordered, not giving Billy a chance to protest before he flung it at him. Billy mumbled something then picked the ladder and moved it towards the door.

"That's not where Mrs. Malcolm wanted us to hang it," Jack corrected. "I don't care," Billy said dryly. He held the small sprig of mistletoe in one hand and a piece of string in the other.

He reached up and secured the mistletoe to the top of the door frame with the string, making sure it was perfectly centered. He stepped back to admire his handiwork, a smile spreading across his face as he looked at the small cluster of green leaves and white berries.

Just then, Sussie walked in and clapped her hands together in excitement. "Oh, it looks fantastic here already! Thank you so much for your help, Jack."

Jack forced a smile and nodded. Billy cleared his throat, "I also helped," he muttered. She raised her head to face him, "ouu Sussie's under the mistletoe, she has to kiss Billy," Isabella cooed.

Sussie stuttered as she looked around, momentarily confused, she looked up at Billy who was just smiling at her. "Oh, please it's a silly Christmas myth," she said then spun around. "Isa, Tim, why don't you go help Miranda with the lights outside?"

"Sure thing, Sus," Tim replied. "I'm coming too," Jack said and left the sitting room. As they walked outside, he let out a sigh of relief. At least he wouldn't have to deal with Sussie for a little while.

"So, what's your deal with Sussie anyway? She's not that bad," Tim said.

"I don't know, we just don't get along. She likes me and I don't like her…"

Tim shrugged and they continued their walk in silence.

They continued stringing lights around the windows and door frames. As they worked, Jack couldn't help but think about how much he wished he were anywhere but there.

When they finished, they went back inside to finish the rest of the decorations. Sussie had set up the tree and was busy putting ornaments on it.

"Do you need help with anything else?" Jack asked.

"No, I think we're good. You guys can go home if you want. I'll take care of the rest," she said.

Jack didn't need to be told twice. He grabbed his coat and headed for the door, Billy following close behind.

When they got home Jack was about to rush to his room when Miranda called him. "Jack, we are having dinner tonight," she started. He looked at her with arched eyebrows, she sighed. "I know you're always going out these days so I'm telling you, you can't go today.".

"Why? It's not like I'm hungry."

"It's a family dinner, everyone will be there, you have to be there, so we can all bond as a family."

"Well, I promised my… girlfriend I was going to meet up with her."

Miranda's eyes lit up with excitement, "are you and Sussie dating?"

"What? No!" He defended, "Her name is Amelia." Miranda's smile weakened but she was still happy, nonetheless. "Perfect! Let her come over then." Jack groaned, "I didn't tell her about this and you know they're around, they'll make her feel uncomfortable."

"Don't speak about your family members like that. If she's not coming over then that's fine but you're having dinner with us," she said with finality and walked away.

Jack sat on his bed, phone in hand, as he texted his girlfriend, he informed her about the change of events, he apologized deeply, and hoped he could make it up to her. But much to his surprise she was excited to have dinner with his family. He let out a sigh of relief.

He was made of flour, sugar, and spices. He had no soul, no heart, no feelings. He was just baked goods; this is what he thought of himself. As nothing but an insignificant gingerbread.

This realization hit Mr. Muller hard. He felt lost and confused. He wanted answers, but nobody in the village seemed to have any. So, he decided to venture into the unknown.

He set off on a journey to find Wong, one of the oldest gingerbread people who lived in isolation in the woods. Mr. Muller was scared, but he was determined.

He trudged through the dense forest, his breath coming in short gasps as he pushed through the underbrush. He had been hiking for hours, and the rugged terrain was taking its toll on his aging body. Despite the hardships, he pressed on, determined to find Wong.

The forest was eerily silent, save for the rustling of leaves and the occasional snap of a twig underfoot. Mr. Muller's senses were on high alert, his eyes scanning the trees for any sign of movement. He had a deep respect for nature, and the thought of being lost in the woods filled him with dread. The only thing keeping him going was the knowledge that he wanted to acquire.

As he ascended a small hill, he caught sight of a clearing in the distance. He quickened his pace, hope blooming in his chest. Perhaps he had finally found Wong's abode. He emerged from the trees, squinting against the bright sun, and took in the scene before him.

The clearing was small, no more than a few hundred feet across, and was surrounded by tall, swaying grasses. Some shuffling noises came from the center, so he naturally assumed it was probably someone. He hesitated for a moment, trying to get a better look, but before he could take a step forward, a branch snapped underfoot.

The group turned as one, and Mr. Muller saw that they were not people at all, but a pack of wild wolves. Their yellow eyes gleamed in the sunlight, and they bared their teeth, growling softly. Mr. Muller's heart raced as he realized his mistake. He had entered their territory, and they were not receptive.

Slowly, he backed away, trying to keep his movements smooth and non-threatening. The wolves watched him, their gazes never leaving his face. Mr. Muller was no stranger to danger, but the ferocity in their eyes was unlike anything he had ever seen. He knew that one false move could mean the end for him.

Just as he was about to turn and run, a flash of movement caught his eye. A figure stumbled out of the trees on the other side of the clearing, looking dazed, injured, and disorientated. The wolves had noticed him too and were starting to close in.

Mr. Muller was torn. He could try to fight off the wolves and save the injured person, but he knew the odds were against him. He could also run and save himself, but he couldn't bear the thought of leaving the other man to die. In the end, his instinct to protect won out, and he stepped forward, shouting to get the wolves' attention.

The pack turned as one, their growls growing louder. Mr. Muller raised his arms, trying to make himself appear larger and more intimidating. The wolves hesitated, he made random sounds and picked up a twig, throwing it with all his might at one of the wolves, its squirm deterred a few others. He rushed and picked up another twig.

The injured person had fallen to the ground, too stunned to move, and Mr. Muller had to keep his attention divided between the wolves and the man. With each passing moment, he grew more exhausted, and he knew that he couldn't keep this up for much longer.

Just as he was about to be overwhelmed, a shot echoed through the clearing. The wolves scattered, yelping in terror as they disappeared back into the trees. Mr. Muller sagged against a tree trunk breathing heavily. He looked over his shoulders towards the direction of the bang.

A man was standing on top of a fallen log of wood, the nozzle of his gun was still smoking and the gun was trained towards the direction the wolves were before they all ran away. The man lowered his gun and began walking towards them.

"Thank you," Muller mouthed. "Hello, young gingerbread," Wong said, ignoring his appreciation. "What brings you to my home?"

Muller's eyes widened, "you're Mr. Wong?"

Wong nodded, "the one and only."

"I am searching for answers," Mr. Muller replied. "I need to know who I am and what my purpose is in this world."

Wong nodded understandingly. "You have come to the right place," he said. "But first let's treat your friend." He pointed to the man sprawled on the floor. Muller nodded in agreement. They both carried him to Wong's home, and Wong used some traditional medicine on him.

When he was done he turned to face Muller, "You taking the risk and the inconvenience to come this far in search of me means you discovered something," Wong started.

"Yes, and I want more clarification."

He sighed, "I have lived for many centuries and have learned much about the world and its secrets. In fact, I had to leave Candland because I just couldn't fit in."

"Please, can you tell me what I am?" Mr. Muller asked.

Wong took a deep breath and began to speak. "You are a gingerbread man, created by the hands of bakers with the intention of being enjoyed. You are not alive, you do not have a soul, but you can bring joy to those who eat you. That is your purpose."

Mr. Muller was shocked. He had never thought of himself as a baked good before. He had always thought of himself as a person, with thoughts and feelings and a soul.

"But what about our lives?" Mr. Muller asked. "Do they mean anything?"

Wong smiled again. "They mean what you make of them," he said. "You may not have a soul, but you can bring joy and happiness to others. That is a gift, and it is something to be proud of."

The doorbell rang and Jack quickly volunteered to get it, hoping it was Amelia. As he pulled the door, she appeared on the other side, dressed moderately in a simple gown. He smiled at her and pulled her into a gentle hug. He was about to kiss her when she moved her head away and greeted his mother. "Good evening mam," she said as her cheeks turned into a bright shade of pink.

"Oh, hello dear, you must be Amelia," she replied with a wide smile. "Yes, I am." Jack stepped aside to allow her to enter the house. "If they try to sike you out, ignore them," Jack whispered into her ears and she chuckled. Miranda eyed them suspiciously.

Amelia nervously adjusted her dress as she approached the rest of the family. This was the first time she would be meeting his family. She had heard so much about them from Jack, and she was eager to finally put a face to the names.

As she stepped into the living room, Amelia was greeted by the rest of Jack's family.

"It's great to finally meet you, Amelia," Victor said, shaking her hand.

"Yes, Jack has told us so much about you," Tim added.

Isabella, who was still in her teenage years, gave her a shy smile. "Hi, Amelia. It's nice to meet you."

Amelia felt a wave of relief wash over her. Everyone was so friendly, and she could tell that they were genuinely happy to meet her.

The family sat down for dinner, and the conversation flowed easily. Amelia was nervous at first, but she quickly relaxed as she got to know Jack's family. They were all warm and welcoming, and she felt like she had known them for years.

"So why date Jack? Of all the boys in Candland" Billy said. Jack clenched his jaw as he stabbed his food aggressively, trying his best not to let his cousin get on his nerves. Amelia chuckled as she placed her palms on his legs to calm him down, noticing his obvious discomfort. "Because I love him," she said softly. She could feel his tensed muscles loosen up.

"So, Amelia, would you like to attend a Christmas Eve party?" Lisa asked. Jack coughed, "No she would not." Amelia's eyes widened, "of course, I would love to come." Jack muttered cusses under his breath, he already hated the idea of the party and he definitely didn't want Sussie and Amelia to ever meet.

"Don't be a party pooper, Jack," Miranda joked, she turned to face Amelia, "I can help you pick an outfit if you'd like." Amelia thanked her but politely declined.

As they ate, Jack's mother asked Amelia about her family and her interests. Amelia talked about her parents and how she loved to read and paint in her free time.

Tim told a funny story about a misadventure he had had with Jack when they were younger, and Isabella shared some of her dreams and ambitions.

As the meal progressed, Amelia felt more and more comfortable. She was amazed at how easy it was to talk to Jack's family. They were all so kind and interesting.

After dinner, the family retired to the living room for coffee and dessert. Jack sat next to Amelia on the couch, holding her hand and smiling at her.

"You did great, Amelia," he whispered. "I told you they would love you."

Amelia smiled back, feeling a warm glow in her chest. "I can see why you are so close to them. They're amazing people."

As the evening went on, Amelia found herself laughing and chatting with Jack's family. She felt like she had known them for years, and she couldn't believe how easy it was to get along with them.

Before she knew it, it was time to go. Jack's mother hugged her as she said goodbye. "It was so nice to meet you, Amelia. You're a wonderful young woman, and I can see why Jack is so taken with you."

Amelia blushed, feeling a warm glow in her chest. "It was great to meet you too, mam. Thank you so much for having me."

As she and Jack left the house, Amelia felt a sense of happiness and belonging. She couldn't believe how well the evening had gone, and she was grateful to Jack's family for making her feel so welcome.

Chapter Ten

Gregory was assigned to accompany Officer Jenkins on a patrol through the city. He was thrilled to finally get some more hands-on experience in the field, and he was eager to see more of what the job was really like.

As they drove through the city, Gregory was amazed by the diversity of the communities they encountered. He saw the challenges that people faced on a daily basis, and he was inspired by the officers' dedication to serving and protecting them.

During the patrol, they received a call about a potential break-in at a local store. Gregory and Officer Jenkins responded quickly, and they soon arrived at the scene.

Gregory was amazed by how quickly and efficiently Officer Jenkins assessed the situation. He was able to determine that there had indeed been a break-in, and he secured the scene for the detectives to investigate. Gregory was impressed by how calm and professional Officer Jenkins remained, even in a high-pressure situation like this.

As they waited for the detectives to arrive, Gregory had the opportunity to talk to the store owner and some of the witnesses. He was able to gather information and assist in the investigation, and he was proud to be a part of the team.

By the time they arrived back at the station, Gregory walked into the squad room, feeling a mixture of excitement and apprehension. He had just finished his first patrol with veteran officer Jenkins, and he was eager to hear what his supervisor, Marai, had to say about his performance.

As he approached her desk, he couldn't help but feel nervous. Marai was known for being strict, and he didn't want to disappoint her. But as he got closer, he realized that there was something about her that he couldn't quite put his finger on. It was a feeling that he had never experienced before, and it made his heart race.

"Good afternoon, Marai," he said, trying to sound as confident as possible.

Marai looked up from her paperwork and smiled. "Good morning, Gregory. How was your patrol with Officer Jenkins?"

"It was great, thanks," Gregory replied. "I learned a lot from him."

"I'm sure you did," Marai said. "And from the report that I just received from Officer Jenkins, it sounds like you held your own out there. He had nothing but praise for you."

Gregory felt a rush of pride. He had worked hard to prove himself, and it was gratifying to hear that his efforts had paid off.

"Thank you, Marai," he said. "I'm glad that I was able to make a good impression."

Marai nodded. "You did more than make a good impression, Gregory. You showed initiative and a real desire to learn, and that's something that I look for in all of my officers."

Gregory felt a warm feeling in his chest, and he suddenly realized that he was in love with Marai. He had never felt this way about anyone before, and he didn't know what to do. He couldn't tell her, of course. She was his supervisor, and he was just an intern. But he couldn't help the way he felt.

"Um, Marai," he said, stumbling over his words. "I just wanted to say that I really respect you and I appreciate everything that you do for the department. You're a great leader and a true inspiration to me."

Marai smiled, looking a little taken aback. "Thank you, Gregory. That means a lot to me."

Gregory felt a knot in his stomach, knowing that he couldn't say anything more. He didn't want to ruin the good impression that he had made, and he didn't want to jeopardize his future with the department.

"Well, I should get back to work," he said, turning to leave. "Thanks again, Marai."

"You're welcome, Gregory," Marai said. "Keep up the good work."

Gregory left the squad room, feeling both relieved and disappointed. He had wanted to tell Marai how he felt, but he knew that he couldn't. He would just have to keep his feelings to himself and do his best to make a name for himself in the department.

As he walked down the hallway, he couldn't help but think about Marai. He was in love with her, and he didn't know what to do about it. But he also knew that he couldn't let his feelings get in the way of his work. He was an intern and he had a job to do. And he was determined to do it to the best of his ability, no matter how he felt.

At the end of his shift, he was already excited to head over to Jack's house to inform him about the new development.

Gregory arrived at Jack's house, feeling nervous and excited. He had been thinking about Marai, his crush, the entire way here and he needed to talk to someone about it. Jack was his best friend, and he trusted him completely.

As he walked up to the front door, he took a deep breath and knocked. A few seconds later, the door opened, and Jack appeared with a huge smile on his face. "Hey man, come on in," he said, stepping aside to let Gregory in.

Gregory walked into the living room and sat down on the couch. Jack sat down next to him, and they chatted for a few minutes about their week. "So, you two are now officially a couple?"

Jack nodded with a sense of pride, "Woah that's nice, you got a love life going for ya." They both chuckled. "How about you? Found love yet?" The smile on Gregory's face widened as Jack spoke, Marai was the only one that came into his mind. Jack's eyes widened, "who's she!?" He asked excitedly.

"Well, there is someone and I think I like her," he said, his voice shaking slightly.

"Who?"

" Marai," Gregory said, his voice barely above a whisper.

"Your supervisor at work?" Jack asked, his eyebrows raised in surprise.

Gregory nodded. "Yeah, I have a crush on her and it's getting out of hand. I can't stop thinking about her, and it's affecting my work."

Jack nodded understandingly. "I know what you mean. Crushes can be tough, especially when they're your boss."

Gregory sighed. "I know, but it's not just that. I feel like I can't do anything right when she's around. I get so nervous, and I can't focus on anything else. I'm afraid I'm going to mess up and she'll realize I'm not cut out for this job."

"Hey, don't worry about that," Jack said, patting Gregory on the back. "You're a great guy, and you're doing a fantastic job at the police station. Marai sees that I'm sure of it."

Gregory shook his head. "I don't know. Sometimes I feel like she's not impressed with me at all. Like she's just tolerating me because I'm an intern."

"That's not true," Jack said firmly. "She wouldn't have hired you if she didn't think you had potential. And even if she doesn't like you romantically, she still respects you as a colleague."

Gregory nodded, feeling a little better. "I guess you're right. But what do I do about these feelings I have for her? I can't just ignore them."

"You have to be careful," Jack warned. "Office romances can be tricky, especially when one person is the boss. You don't want to jeopardize your job or make things awkward between the two of you."

"I know," Gregory said. "But I can't help how I feel. I just want to be with her, to make her happy."

"Well, you have to think about what's best for both of you," Jack said. "If you think there's a chance that things could work out between the two of you, then go for it. But if you're not sure, it's probably better to keep your feelings to yourself for now."

Gregory nodded, feeling a little disappointed but also relieved. Jack was right, he couldn't just act on his feelings without thinking about the consequences. He needed to be careful.

The two of them talked for a little while longer, and then Gregory got up to leave. "Thanks for talking to me, Jack," he said, feeling grateful for his friend.

The man woke up in a strange room, the walls were made of hand candy, and the only source of light was a small window that let in the morning sun. He tried to move his body but felt a sharp pain in his shoulder. He let out a groan, which was heard by Mr Muller who was sitting on a chair by his bedside.

Mr. Muller jumped up and approached him, "Good morning, you're finally awake. I'm Mr. Muller, I ran into you in the woods, badly injured, you passed out while some wolves were trying to attack us," he said in a calm and friendly tone.

The man tried to recall how he got there, but his memories were vague. "What happened?" he asked in confusion as he strained his neck to look around.

"We'll get to that, but first, let me introduce you to Wong. He's been taking care of you since I brought you here," Mr. Muller said, gesturing to Wong who had just entered the room.

Wong approached the bed and smiled warmly, "Hello, I'm Wong. How are you feeling today?"

"I'm in pain, but I'll survive. You're the one that shot those wolves, I vaguely remember seeing you hold a gun before I passed out," the man replied, trying to sit up but the pain was too much.

Wong gently pushed him back down, "Don't try to move too much, you need to rest," he said, his voice filled with concern. "Yes, the good ol' icing powder and caramel bullets," he said with wide pride in his voice.

The man nodded, "Where am I? How did I get here?"

Mr. Muller and Wong exchanged a look, then Mr. Muller said, "We don't know, we were hoping you'd tell us, firstly what's your name?"

"John. All I remember was that I went hiking with some friends and this shiny… beast descended and began to snatch them. I managed to escape but it hit me and I tumbled down a hill."

Miller's eyes widened in shock, "A beast? Could that be what's responsible for the mysterious disappearances?"

"Indeed, a few who have survived the ordeal have similar stories," Wong confirmed.

John shook his head, "That's impossible, it must be a nightmare," he said, but deep down, he knew it was real.

"I assure you, it's not a nightmare," Wong said, his voice serious, "you've seen it with your own eyes, and many others have too."

The man's thoughts raced, he tried to remember what happened, but all he could recall was a bright light and a sense of falling, getting up and encountering wolves, then nothing until he woke up in this room.

Muller placed a hand on his shoulder, "Do you remember anything about the attack? Anything that could help us understand what's going on?"

The man closed his eyes and focused, then a memory came to him, "I remember a bright light, then I saw people lifted into the air and others being taken too, but I don't remember anything after that."

"That's all you remember?" Mr. Muller asked, his eyebrows furrowed.

The man nodded, "Yes, that's all I can recall, my girlfriend was taken, I wish I died too, why was I spared?"

Wong and Mr. Muller exchanged a look, then Mr. Muller said, "We don't know, but we believe you were meant to survive, to spread the word and help us find a way to stop this monster."

The man was filled with a sense of purpose, he nodded, "I'll do what I can to help."

Wong and Mr. Muller smiled, "Good, now rest, and when you're feeling better we should head back to Candland, maybe the police department would have something to say," Muller suggested. Wong remained indifferent as he stared at the skies through the window.

Sussie's house was buzzing with excitement as the Christmas Eve party got underway. The large, sprawling property was lit up with strings of twinkling lights, creating a warm and inviting atmosphere. The crisp, cool winter air was filled with the sounds of laughter, music, and the clinking of glasses.

The street in front of Sussie's house was bustling with activity. Cars were parked haphazardly on both sides of the road, some with their engines still running and others with their headlights shining. The sound of cheerful chatter and car doors slamming filled the air as guests arrived for the party. People hugged each other and walked up the driveway, carrying gifts and bags of food. The lawn was illuminated by twinkling Christmas lights, casting a warm glow over the festive scene.

The party was being held in Sussie's backyard, which was spacious enough to accommodate the large crowd of guests. The lawn was covered with a layer of freshly fallen snow, making it the perfect backdrop for the festive occasion. At the center of the yard was a giant Christmas tree, standing tall and proud with its branches decorated with ornaments and tinsel.

Guests were milling about, chatting, and enjoying each other's company. Some were gathered around the outdoor fire pit, roasting marshmallows, and sipping on hot cocoa. Others were dancing to the lively tunes being played by a local band, who had set up their instruments on a stage at one end of the yard.

A large dining area had been set up near the house, where a sumptuous feast was being served. The smell of roasted turkey, honey-glazed ham, and a variety of other delicious dishes wafted through the air, making everyone's mouth water. There were also tables upon tables of sweets and desserts, including Christmas cookies, fruitcakes, and a towering gingerbread house.

Sussie's mother, the host of the party, was in her element, greeting guests and making sure everyone was having a good time. She was dressed in a festive red and green outfit, with a Santa hat perched jauntily on her head. Her bright smile and infectious laughter had a way of making everyone feel at ease.

Jack walked into Sussie's house for the Christmas Eve party, dressed in his old-school outfit. He wore a classic fedora hat in black, a crisp white shirt with the sleeves rolled up to his elbows, a pair of high-waisted, wide-legged trousers in a soft gray, and a pair of glossy black oxford shoes. He also wore a vintage black leather jacket, adding a touch of edge to his look. As he walked in, the rest of his family followed behind him.

He was constantly checking his phone to see if Amelia had arrived. "Merry Christmas!" Sussie greeted them. Billy smiled sheepishly at her.

Tim and Isabella instinctively headed to the yard where most of the other teenagers were.

Sussie's eyes trailed Jack as he walked towards the couch to have a seat, she took in a deep breath and adjusted her dress with her arms then approached him. "Hey Jack," she called. He barely turned his head around to acknowledge her presence but he responded. "How are you?"

"I'm fine, look Jack I'm sorry about what happened-"

"It's okay, I'm sorry for being harsh too, let's just put it behind us, we've been good friends for a long time, let's not ruin that." She nodded in agreement, even though she wanted much more. She was about to open her mouth to speak when Jack's phone buzzed, he jumped on his feet excitedly. "What? Are you expecting someone?" She asked, with slight amusement in her tone. "Yes, see you later," he said politely before heading out. Sussie eyed him suspiciously and then got up, deciding to go after him.

Jack walked out of the building and met Amelia on the lawn, she was styled in a classic 1920s style flapper dress. The black beaded dress shimmered in the moonlight and featured a fringe hemline that grazed the top of her ankles. To complete the look, Amelia added a bright red beret and a diamond necklace. She accessorized her outfit with a pair of black patent leather pumps and a red clutch. Her hair was done up in a vintage finger-wave style, giving her a timeless look. As she walked up the porch steps, Amelia was filled with confidence and ready to show off her old-school look. She received several glances and compliments as she approached Jack.

"Hey?" She said, waving her arms at a gawking Jack. "You're so beautiful," he whispered and pulled her into a deep kiss. Just then Sussie came out of the house, and much to her shock, ran into her crush making out with another girl. She clenched her fists in anger and stormed back into the party.

Shortly after, Gregory and a few other officers and interns from the police department came over. As the night wore on, the party showed no signs of slowing down. More guests arrived, bringing with them a fresh burst of energy. The music grew louder, the laughter grew more boisterous, and the dance floor became more crowded. It was a magical evening, filled with the joy and excitement of the holiday season.

The backyard was transformed into a winter wonderland, with ice sculptures and snowmen dotted about. Children were playing games, building snow forts, and sliding down an improvised snow-covered hill on their sleds.

Jack walked up to Amelia with a glass of eggnog in his hand, "Hey, want some?" She shook her head slowly, "I'm getting a bit dizzy, maybe it's the eggnog. I think I need to lie down." Jack quickly put his cup down, "My house is just down the street, I could take you there to rest."

"What? And have you miss out on this party? No Jack, I'll just rest on the couch or something."

"Baby, you look stressed c'mon let's go." Her stomach performed a sharp maneuver upon hearing him call her that, she smiled to herself and looked at him. "You'll miss the countdown with your family and friends," she said, trying to convince him. "You also left your family and friends to come here, and besides I don't like this party."

He got up and gently dragged her towards the front door. "Where are you two going?" Sussie's voice rang from behind. Amelia turned around, slightly confused. "Jack, who's this?" Sussie asked. He sighed before responding, "My girlfriend."

His words knocked the air straight out of her lungs, she could feel her knees buckle under her weight and her stomach as it twisted in tight knots. "Amelia, meet Sussie, my friend... and the daughter of the people hosting this party," he added. Amelia smiled and extended her arm for a handshake but Sussie left it hanging as she eyed it with mild disgust. She slowly retracted her arm and turned to look at Jack. "Alright, we were just on our way out," Jack informed.

"But the party isn't over yet... What about the countdown to Christmas?" Amelia grew nervous as she watched the interaction between the two. "We'll pass," he replied and left with Amelia.

"What was that?" Amelia asked once they were on the street, far from the bustling party. "She's just like that, just ignore her."

He opened the door to his house and Amelia followed him in, he took her to his room and made sure she laid down on the bed to get some much-needed rest.

Back at the party, as midnight approached, everyone gathered around the Christmas tree, waiting for the countdown to begin. The excitement in the air was palpable as everyone sang carols and waited for the moment to strike. And when it finally did, the crowd erupted into cheers, wishing each other a Merry Christmas, and ringing in the holiday season in style.

The party continued well into the night, with guests spilling out into the house as they took a break from the festivities. Sussie's home was filled with the sounds of music, laughter, and good cheer. It was a Christmas Eve party to remember, and everyone agreed that it was the perfect way to kick off the holiday season.

As the party finally began to wind down, guests said their goodbyes and headed out into the cool winter night. They were filled with joy, having shared an unforgettable evening with friends and family. And as they stepped out into the street, they were greeted by a blanket of snow, a reminder of the special night they had just experienced.

Sussie's Christmas Eve party was a resounding success, with guests leaving filled with the spirit of the season and already looking forward to next year's festivities. It was a night that would be remembered for years to come, a night that brought together friends and family, and a night that truly embodied the magic of the holiday season.

Amelia crept down the quiet, dark street, trying to be as silent as possible. The party she had attended last night had been wild and unforgettable, but now, as she made her way back home, all she could think about was the consequences of her actions. She was sure her parents were going to be furious when they found out that she had snuck out, and that thought made her heart race with fear.

As she approached her house, she realized that she had left her keys in Jack's room. Now, she was going to have to find a way to get inside without waking up her parents. She glanced around, searching for any sign of a spare key or an open window, but there was nothing. She was going to have to get creative.

Amelia walked around to the back of the house and found a trellis that led up to her bedroom window. She had climbed it many times before, but never in the early hours of the mourning while trying to be quiet. She took a deep breath and began to climb, her heart pounding in her chest.

She had made it halfway up the trellis when she heard a creak from below. She froze, holding her breath and listening for any sign of her parents. She heard nothing, so she continued on, her heart racing even faster.

Finally, she reached her window and gently pushed it open. She climbed inside and silently closed the window behind her. She let out a sigh of relief, but she wasn't out of the woods yet. She still had to make it to her bed without waking her parents.

She tiptoed across the room, her heart pounding in her chest. She was so focused on being quiet that she didn't see the pile of clothes on the floor until she had tripped over them. She let out a small yelp as she fell, but she quickly covered her mouth with her hand, praying that her parents hadn't heard her.

She lay there for what felt like an eternity, listening for any sign that she had been caught. When she heard nothing, she slowly got to her feet and continued on to her bed. She climbed in, pulled the covers up to her chin, and let out a long, deep sigh of relief.

As she lay there in the dark, she realized that she had made it back home without getting caught. She chuckled to herself as she jumped on her bed excitedly. She quickly pulled out her phone and texted Jack.

I made it home - at 4:01 AM

She dropped the phone on her nightstand and began to undress, she changed into pajamas and decided to get a good night's rest.

Chapter Eleven

Amelia groaned as she opened her eyes. She felt like her head was splitting in two and the weakness that followed told her that she definitely had a bit too much to drink.

She looked at the clock on her nightstand. It was already half past nine, she usually never woke up this late. She grabbed her phone to text Jack.

A wide smile spread across her face when a notification from him popped up, they texted each other briefly before she decided to get out of bed, she locked her phone and sat erect on her bed, taking in a deep relaxing breath.

They began to discuss how they would spend the afternoon together and Amelia decided to go downstairs to get some water to drink. As she hurriedly went down the stairs she heard her father harrumph by the corner, with a glass of fruit wine in his hands.

She turned around to face him, "Hey Dad, good morning." He scoffed and got on his feet, "there's nothing good about the morning Amelia," he said, his voice void of a friendly tone.

She froze in her tracks, confused by her father's countenance. Rodolfo walked over to her and said in a stern voice, "Where were you last night Amelia?"

His words penetrated into her, sending shivers down her spine. She hung her head, unable to look her father in the eyes. "I know you went to see that low-life scum Jack; you left your mother and I on Christmas Eve to get see that-"

"Dad, he's a good person!" She yelled, letting her rash impulses take over her better judgment. He looked at her with a crease on his forehead. "Are you talking back to me?" He asked in a low threatening tone.

"I'm not talking back, I'm having a normal conversation, like adults do. I'm not a child anymore."

He clenched his jaw and neared her. "That does it!" He raised his arms to smack her across the face but Sarah quickly grasped his wrist. "Rodolfo!" She cautioned.

He looked over his shoulders at her and snatched his arm away from her hold. He turned to look at his daughter, his eyes resembling a lit furnace, "You are grounded, you are not allowed to leave this house, nor are you allowed to have visitors."

"But-"

"That's enough!" Sarah interjected, "Listen to your father and go to your room now!" Amelia looked between the two before scoffing loudly and running back up the stairs. She opened her room door and quickly slammed it shut behind her.

She rushed to her bed, diving face down on it as she began to sob.

Jack locked his phone screen when he realized that Amelia wasn't replying, and decided it was best to head downstairs for breakfast. Jack sat at the kitchen table, surrounded by his family. Victor and Miranda were busy dishing out pancakes and bacon, while Tim played with his phone. His grandmother sat at the head of the table, sipping on her coffee.

"So, Jack, how's life treating you these days?" his grandmother asked.

"It's going well, Grandma," Jack replied, trying to hide the frustration in his voice. He knew what was coming next. Miranda eyed him from afar, signaling to him that he should not be rude.

"That's good to hear," his grandmother said, "I was just talking to Billy the other day. He's doing so well at university. I'm so proud of him."

"That's great," Jack said dryly. "You know my boy Billy is even on his school's front-page picture," Lisa added. Jack rolled his eyes so hard that they threatened to fall out.

"When are you going to follow in his footsteps and get a good education, Jack?"

Jack sighed. This was a conversation he had many times before with his grandmother. "I'm taking my time, Grandma. I'm just figuring out what I want to do with my life."

His grandmother snorted. "Well, time is running out, Jack. You're not getting any younger, you know. Billy's already making a name for himself and you're just sitting around doing nothing. What are you going to do with your life?"

At the mention of his name, Billy, who was sitting next to Jack, couldn't help but smile with pride.

Jack's parents exchanged a quick look but remained silent. Jack took a deep breath and tried to keep his voice calm. "I appreciate your concern, Grandma. But I have to make my own decisions and figure out what's best for me. And right now, that's not my priority. I have a job-"

"You called that a job?!" She cackled. "A few years from now Billy would be working a white collared job, and what would you be doing? Working shifts in a bakeshop?"

"I don't plan to work there forever."

"Yeah right," she snorted. Jack let his spoon clang on his plate as he stood up abruptly and walked away. "Jack!" Miranda called, but he ignored her.

"What a rude kid," his grandmother said. He couldn't wait for the Christmas season to be over so the extended family could go back to their house.

It was a crisp winter morning and Mr. Muller, Wong, and John were walking towards the police station, eager to report the absurd beasts they had seen in the woods the previous night. The three were determined to make sure that others were made aware of the danger that was lurking in the woods and Candland as well.

Mr. Muller recounted the events. He described how he was attacked by wolves, and how John was injured when he was running away from the strange beasts, when Wong found them and shot them.

"I thought it was just an animal rustling the leaves in the canopies at first," John said. "But then the noise got louder and closer, and that's when I saw it. It was unlike anything I had ever seen before. It was massive, at least eight feet tall, descending from the sky and I was frozen with fear."

Wong nodded in agreement. "I have never seen anything like it before and it abducted those other people, I was the only survivor," he said.

The policewoman looked up, her expression changing to one of concern when she saw the look of fear on John's face. "Are you certain this... creatures' those people?"

John nodded.

Marai looked over her shoulders at Officer Jenkins, "we need to inform the chief about this, this might be linked to all the other disappearances," she said. Jenkins looked at her doubtfully.

"Look that could explain the unexplained scratch marks on the road," she said in a hushed tone. He began to ponder deeply on the possibility of what Marai was proposing.

They assured the trio that it would be looked into and with that, the three left the station.

Marai was assigned to lead the investigation following the reports of strange activities in the woods near the outskirts of town. She was determined to uncover the truth and was hopeful that this was linked to the disappearances.

As she walked into the smaller offices, Marai was greeted by Gregory.

"Good morning, Detective," Gregory said, offering a salute.

"Good morning, Intern," Marai replied with a smile. "I'm glad you're here today. We've got a big case to work on."

Marai briefed him on the situation, explaining that they were going to investigate the woods near the town's border. She told him about the strange sightings.

He was fascinated and couldn't wait to get started. He saw this as another chance to prove himself to Marai yet again.

"Let's go," Marai said, grabbing her coat and leading the way to their squad car.

As they drove towards the woods, she filled him in on the details of the case. She explained that they were going to search the area for any DNA or marks.

"We'll start by interviewing some farmers who live around the region," she said. "And then we'll take a closer look at the woods themselves, see if we can find anything out of the ordinary."

Jack heard the doorbell ring and he sighed. He wasn't in the mood for visitors, but he couldn't ignore the door. He walked over and opened it, and his heart sank when he saw who was standing on the other side. It was Sussie. Jack had never been able to put his finger on why, but there was just something about her that irked him.

"Hi Jack," Sussie said, a fake smile plastered on her face.

"What are you doing here?" Jack asked, trying to keep his tone neutral.

"I just came to see Billy," Sussie replied, brushing past him, and entering the house.

Jack was taken aback, he never thought she would come over unannounced just to see Billy as the two had only met each other a few times. He followed her into the living room, where Billy was watching TV.

"Hey, what's up- Sussie?" Billy said, looking up from the TV, he was shocked to see her.

"Sussie just stopped by to say hi," Jack said, trying to hide his annoyance.

"Awesome!" Billy said, jumping up from the couch. "What brings you here?"

"I just wanted to check in and see how you're doing," Sussie said, giving Billy a flirtatious smile.

Jack rolled his eyes. He didn't like how Sussie was acting around his cousin. He knew that Billy was a good guy, despite how unbearably annoying he was, but he also knew that he could be a bit naive when it came to women. Jack didn't want to see his cousin get hurt, especially not by someone like Sussie.

"Well, it was nice of you to stop by," Jack said, trying to usher Sussie towards the door. "But I'm sure you have other things to do."

"Oh, I have a little time," Sussie said, sitting down on the couch next to Billy.

Jack sighed. He didn't know what to do. He didn't want to be rude, but he also didn't want Sussie to stay any longer than she had to. He decided to give in and let her stay, at least for a little while.

The three of them made small talk for a while, but Jack found it hard to concentrate. He was still thinking about why Sussie had come over in the first place. He couldn't shake the feeling that there was something she wasn't telling them.

"Is your mom home?" She asked. "No, she went downtown," Billy replied.

Finally, Sussie got up to leave. "In that case, I should get going," she said. "It was great seeing you guys."

"It was great seeing you too," Billy said, giving her a hug. Jack forced a smile and walked her to the door. "Take care," he said as she walked out. His eyes didn't leave her retreating back.

As soon as the door was closed, Jack turned to Billy. "What was that all about?" he asked.

"What do you mean?" Billy said, looking confused.

"Sussie," Jack said. "Why did she come over here?"

"I don't know," Billy said, shrugging. "She just wanted to see me, I guess."

"I don't buy it," Jack said. "There's something she's not telling us."

"What are you talking about?" Billy asked.

"I don't know," Jack said. "But she's up to something."

The two of them sat in silence for a moment, both lost in thought. Finally, Billy spoke up. "I think you're jealous," he said.

"What?" Jack asked.

"Jealous, you're jealous she's finally noticing me."

Jack scoffed, "I have a girlfriend." Billy rolled his eyes, "Maybe you're bothered you're no longer the center of attention."

Having enough of his cousin's nonsense, Jack headed up to his room. He sat down on his bed, letting out a deep sigh as he kicked off his shoes and leaned back into the pillows. It was at that moment that his phone rang. He picked it up, seeing that it was his girlfriend Amelia. He answered, a smile spreading across his face.

"Hey, Amelia," Jack said, happy to hear from her.

"Hey, Jack! How was your day?" Amelia asked, her voice sounding cheerful on the other end of the line.

"It was long but good. How about you?" Jack replied, letting out another deep sigh.

"Same. I just got off work and I was thinking...we haven't seen each other in a while," Amelia said, her tone turning serious.

"We were together yesterday," he teased.

"I know. I miss you," she admitted, feeling a pang of sadness at the thought of not being able to see Jack as often as she would like.

"That's why I was thinking, why don't we meet up tonight?" Amelia suggested, her voice perking up.

"That sounds great! Where do you want to meet?" Jack asked, feeling a sudden rush of excitement.

"My house," Amelia said. Jack went mute, recalling his experience with her father. "I don't think that's a-"

"Jack I know, but please, I'm not allowed to leave the house." Jack chuckled, "You're grounded?"

"I'm serious."

"Okay okay sorry, but wouldn't your parents freak?"

"No, they're going for an outing," she assured.

"Sure, that sounds perfect. What time?" Jack asked.

"How about 6 PM?" Amelia suggested.

"That works for me. I'll see you later," Jack replied, already getting up from his bed to start getting ready.

As he hung up the phone, Jack couldn't help but feel grateful for Amelia's call. He had been feeling so down, but now he had something to look forward to. He quickly got dressed, making sure to pick out his favorite shirt and slacks. He wanted to look his best for Amelia.

Chapter Twelve

Marai and Gregory were deep in the woods, carrying out their investigations. Earlier, they had interviewed some people who dwelled around the area, but nobody seemed to be giving any significant details, except for a garlic farmer who said he had indeed seen some strange things descending very quickly from the sky and abducting people.

As they made their way through the dense underbrush, they suddenly heard a commotion coming from the direction of their backup unit. Rushing towards the source of the noise, they stumbled upon a horrifying scene. Several of their fellow officers were being attacked and snatched from the ground. Jenkins yelled at them to retreat and pulled out his Glock, firing randomly into the canopies as he assumed a lower position.

Marai sprang into action, drawing her sidearm and firing off a warning shot to try and drive the monster away. Gregory, meanwhile, was frozen in terror, unable to move as he watched in horror as some of their fellow officers were attacked.

Marai shouted for Gregory to snap out of it, and together they made a run for the safety of a nearby cave. As they sprinted through the underbrush, Marai radioed for backup, frantically shouting.

"Hello?! All available units, we need backup!"

She turned around and for the first time she caught a glimpse of the beast; it resembled a large blurry streak and when she traced its trajectory with her eyes, her heart skipped a beat.

"Jenkins!!" She screeched at the top of her voice. He was quick to react by somersaulting away from it. But the force caused him to roll into a tree. He groaned in pain as he was sprawled on the ground.

Gregory grabbed Marai by the wrist and yanked her towards the interior of the cave, once in, they took a moment to catch their breath and assess their situation.

Marai's heart was pounding in her chest, and she could feel a cold sweat breaking out on her brow. Gregory, meanwhile, was shaking and white-faced, still in shock from the horrors he had just witnessed.

Marai quickly took charge, barking orders at Gregory to try and get him to focus. She instructed him to guard the entrance of the cave while she tried to contact the backup unit again. Gregory, still in a daze, nodded numbly and took up a position at the mouth of the cave, his hand shaking as he held his firearm.

Marai's efforts to reach backup were in vain, as the radio seemed to be malfunctioning. Frantic, she tried to think of a way to escape the cave and reach safety, but the sound of the footsteps of the other police units running helter-skelter gave away the fact that there was still commotion outside.

With nowhere else to turn, Marai and Gregory huddled in the cave, trying to come up with a plan. "You stay here, I'll go out there and see how I can help."

Gregory shot her an incredulous look, "What!? No! You can't go out there!" He said, standing in front of the passage to block her way.

"I'm the one that's trained to handle these situations so move!" She said, feigning assertiveness in her tone. "No, I won't!"

"Gregory-" she warned in a low tone, "-get out of my way." He spread his arms out to further restrict her movement. "No."

She sighed and tried to push past him but he trapped her arm and drew her back into the cave. "Unhand me this instant, Gregory!"

"I can't!"

"Why?!"

"Because I love you!" His words echoed in the cave, resonating repeatedly in her ears. "I love you and I can't let anything bad happen to you," he added, re-enforcing what she had just heard. She blinked many times as she stood glued to the spot, still trying to process what he said.

The sound of sirens in the distance distracted her, she whipped her head out and saw that some backup had arrived and that it was relatively peaceful, which meant that the beast was gone. They shared a look before both deciding to exit the cave without saying another word.

Marai and Gregory emerged from the cave to see some injured officers being carried on stretchers. They quickly made their way towards the safety of the backup unit, grateful to be alive. Marai quickly went to check on Jenkins, he had suffered minor injuries but was generally alright. "We lost four men," he said to her.

She shook her head slowly, "Well, I guess my hunch was corrected, this thing is linked to the disappearances, remember that statement from the girl who lost one of her dogs to this?"

Jenkins nodded. "This is more serious than we thought," he remarked.

She turned and caught Gregory staring at her intensely as if he was trying to gauge her reaction. She decided to ignore him and mingle with the other officers.

As they rode back to the station, Marai couldn't help but think about how lucky they had been to make it out of the woods alive. She made a mental note to be extra cautious in the future, and to never let her guard down in the face of danger.

Jack was a little nervous as he approached Amelia's house. He didn't know how he was going to act or what to say around her father if he were to come back early. But he pushed the thought to the back of his mind and focused on the positive - he was going to get to spend some time with Amelia.

He knocked on the door and Amelia answered almost immediately, greeting him with a big smile. "Hi Jack!" she said, embracing him in a warm hug.

"Hi Amelia," Jack replied, smiling back. The last time he was here, he never really took the time to appreciate the interior décor.

"Come in," Amelia said, taking his hand and leading him inside.

The house was quiet and Jack could feel the tension in the air. He knew that Amelia's father was always watching and judging him, but for once, Jack didn't have to worry about that. They could just relax and be themselves.

As Jack followed Amelia up the stairs, he noticed the family photos that lined the walls. There were photos of Amelia as a child and more recent photos of the whole family, smiling and happy.

"Amelia, I have something to tell you," Jack said, turning to face her.

"What is it?" she asked, looking up at him with a smile.

"I love you," Jack said, taking her hand in his. "I know we've only been dating for a short time, but I just can't imagine my life without you. I want to spend the rest of my life making you happy."

Tears filled Amelia's eyes as she looked up at Jack. "I love you too," she said, throwing her arms around him.

They hugged each other tightly, lost in their own world. Jack felt like he was on top of the world, he had never been this happy before.

She withdrew herself from their hug and looked him in the eyes, she interlocked her fingers around the base of his neck and pulled him into a deep kiss. He reciprocated the kiss and a soft moan escaped from her. His hands raked over her body, lustfully eliminating any piece of fabric it could touch. She reached for the hem of his shirt and pulled it over his head.

Now unclad, they continued their frivolous adventure, he ran kisses down her neck sending shivers down her spine. She reached for his groin, stroking it passionately as they looked each other in the eyes. He quivered as he shot icing all over her frame, leaving crumbles on the bed.

She guided his shaft inside her, moaning softly as he filled her. They made love like it was their last time, ignoring the consequences.

The days following Christmas were just like another typical day at the police station for Gregory. He and Marai hadn't talked about what happened in the cave, and he didn't want to push his luck by bringing it up. Marai had suggested that he took the day off, but he refused, seeing no need to. He was having a conversation with another intern when suddenly, the calm atmosphere was disrupted by a loud siren, signaling that a report of an emergency had come in.

"Attention all units, we have a report of homes being attacked by monsters on the East side of the city. All available officers, please respond," came the voice over the loudspeaker.

Gregory's heart raced with excitement and fear. He couldn't help but wonder what he might face. He quickly gathered his equipment and ran towards the police vehicles parked outside the station.

As he approached, he saw that several officers were already piling into their cars and revving up the engines. He jogged up to the nearest car and opened the passenger door, hopping in beside the officer behind the wheel.

"Where are we headed?" Gregory asked.

"East side, reports of homes being attacked by monsters," the officer replied.

The car peeled out of the parking lot and quickly joined the procession of police vehicles heading towards the emergency. As they drove, Gregory could see the tension on the faces of the officers in the car. He tried to calm his nerves and focus on the task at hand.

Finally, they arrived at the scene of the emergency. The street was packed with people, all talking and pointing in the direction of the homes that had been attacked. The officers quickly sprang into action, securing the perimeter and assessing the situation.

Gregory followed closely behind the officers as they approached one of the homes that had been attacked. The front door was hanging off its hinges and there was a large hole in the wall. The officers cautiously entered the home, weapons drawn, ready for anything.

Gregory was amazed at the destruction he saw inside. Furniture was overturned, and there were deep gashes in the walls and floor. The officers quickly searched the house and confirmed that no one was inside. They then moved on to the next home.

"What do you think it could be?" Gregory asked Jenkins. "Never seen anything like this before, I don't know." They kicked down the door and began to troop in. "Gregory, I think you should stay outside," Officer Jenkins ordered before entering the building with the other cops. He was a bit disappointed but he complied with the instructions.

As he stood outside he helped guide people towards the ambulance. Then, a little girl standing in the middle of the road caught his attention. He looked up to the sky and what he saw made his blood run cold, towering over her was a sleek and slender lustrous creature gliding through the air. Its powerful jaws opened and closed with a snap, ready to clasp onto anything in its path.

With lightning speed and precise movements, it descended towards the little girl. "No!" He cried as he ran towards the girl, he managed to scoop her away from its path and they both tumbled to a stop by the sidewalk. "Are you okay?" He asked, the girl nodded.

"Gregory!!" A sharp voice called, he whipped his head to the side and saw Marai frantically pointing over his head. By the time he spun around it was too late.

It clamped against his arm with bone-crushing strength and soon he was airborne, the police officers shot relentlessly but their hand-candy bullets did nothing to deter the beast. Gregory struggled to the best of his capacity, but by the time he reached a certain altitude, he froze.

He ascended into the sky with the beast, never to be seen again. Back at the crime scene, panic ensued among everyone, they had finally seen what was causing the disappearances and it was worse than what anyone had envisioned. Marai looked skywards with sadness and disappointment etched on her face.

The funeral of Gregory was a somber affair. A crowd of mourners gathered in the chapel, all dressed in black, their faces etched with sadness. Jack stood at the back of the room; his eyes fixed on the casket which was empty because his best friend's body was gone. He couldn't believe that Gregory was gone. It seemed like only yesterday they were joking around and making plans for the future. Now, those plans would never come to fruition.

The priest began the service, his words a comfort to some, but they did little to ease Jack's pain. He felt numb as if his heart had been ripped from his chest. Gregory had been more than just a friend; he had been a brother. They had grown up together, been there for each other through thick and thin, and now he was gone, leaving Jack with a void that could never be filled.

As the service progressed, Jack remembered all the good times they had shared. The fishing trips, the camping trips, the countless nights spent playing video games and just hanging out. Gregory had been a part of his life for as long as he could remember, and now he was gone, leaving Jack feeling lost and alone.

Amelia could feel the heavy air of sadness that hung over the mourners. She reached out and took Jack's hand, squeezing it reassuringly. "It's going to be okay," she whispered in his ear.

Jack looked up at her with a sad smile, his eyes red and puffy from the tears he had shed. "I just don't know how I'm going to get through this," he said.

Amelia put her arm around him and pulled him close. "I'm here for you," she said. "I'll be here for you every step of the way."

She held Jack's hand tightly throughout. She could feel his pain, and she was determined to be there for him. When the service ended and the mourners began to disperse, Amelia and Jack stayed behind. They stood there in silence, paying their respects.

He approached the casket, staring down at what should have been his friend's peaceful face. He reached out, touching the cold metal, feeling the finality of the moment.

"Goodbye, Gregory," he whispered, tears streaming down his face. "I'll miss you, my brother."

As he turned to leave, he was approached by Gregory's family. His mother hugged him tightly, tears streaming down her face. "Thank you for being here for my son," she said. "He loved you so much, Jack."

Jack hugged her back, feeling her pain as his own. "He was my best friend," he said. "I loved him too."

The family thanked him and moved on to speak with other mourners, leaving Jack standing alone. He took one last look at the casket before turning around and heading out with Amelia.

A few weeks later

Jack was waiting for Amelia at their spot in the woods. Dry leaves crunched under her feet as she approached from behind. "Hey Jack," she called lovingly. He turned around and pulled her into a hug, caressing her waist as he planted a soft kiss on her forehead.

She looked up at him, "How was your shift at the bakeshop?"

"It was sweet," he joked. She snickered softly, catching his humor. "How are you?"

"The usual, my parents keep fighting every now and then... nothing much." He nodded. He reached into his backpack and brought out a small speaker, "do you dance?" He asked. She smiled, "I took dance classes during the summer," she said boastfully.

"I'm trying to find the perfect song for us to dance to, my love," he said.

"As long as we're together, any song will be perfect."

"You're so right. But I want it to be extra special. Let me see... Ah! I think I found it."

The sound of a soft and romantic melody filled the air. Jack took Amelia into his arms and they started dancing slowly to the rhythm.

"It's beautiful. What is it?" Amelia asked.

"It's called 'not alone' by Davy Jones. It's our song, my love."

Amelia smiled and leaned her head on Jack's shoulder, closing her eyes and enjoying the moment. They danced and laughed, lost in their own world.

"I love you, Amelia. I want to spend the rest of my life with you, making memories like this."

"I love you too, Jack. Forever and always." They continued to sway around in near-perfect harmony.

And at that moment, surrounded by the beauty of nature and the sweet sound of music, Jack and Amelia were perfectly happy.

The sun was setting quickly and they knew they needed to leave soon, so they took a selfie before leaving.

"Wait, Jack my earrings... one piece is missing," she said when they had almost gotten to the trailhead. "Should we go back and check?" He suggested.

She was skeptical but she agreed and they headed back. They began to walk around the areas they stayed, leaving no stone unturned in their search. "It has to be here," Amelia whispered to herself.

Just then a branch snapped and she shot her head up. "Jack?"

"Yes?" He called, standing a few feet away from her. "Did you hear that?" He stood upright and began walking towards her, "hear what?"

She was about to respond before the elongated lustrous beast descended, grasping him, and taking him into the skies, right before her very eyes. She screamed at the top of her lungs, quickly growing weak in the knees as she went down, with tears building up in her eyes.

A man dressed in a Santa costume sat by the display, selecting which Human shaped gingerbread he wanted to eat. "I like how each one looks different," he said to the chef. The chef bowed politely, his tray was filled with gingerbreads, pastries, and other candies. He stepped away from the display and dropped the lustrous kitchen tong on the table.

As he took a bite of one of the gingerbreads he groaned, "These are really good," he mumbled with his mouth full.

He cleaned the crumbs on his lips with his sleeves and stood up, "well now that Christmas is over, time to go back to working on the counter," he said before leaving the bakeshop.

The chef sprinkled more grated white chocolate on the gingerbread town to suit the winter aesthetic. He looked at his inanimate creation and walked away, turning off the lights in the shop before clocking out.

Amelia stood at their favorite spot in the woods, the sun filtering through the trees and dappling the ground beneath her feet. She placed a gentle hand over her growing belly, filled with a love and warmth that she knew Jack would have shared with her.

She closed her eyes, remembering the laughter and the joy they shared in this very spot. A smile touched her lips as she imagined his smile and his embrace. She whispered a promise to their baby, that they would always be loved and that Jack would always be remembered.

In this quiet, peaceful place, Amelia felt a sense of closure and a new beginning. She was filled with a sense of purpose as she looked forward to becoming a mother and raising their child with all the love and devotion that Jack would have shown.

Amelia opened her eyes and gazed out at the beauty of the woods, feeling the gentle breeze brush against her skin. She knew that Jack would always be with her in spirit, guiding her and their child on this new journey.

With a deep sense of gratitude and peace, Amelia took one last look at the place that had held so many happy memories and turned to make her way home, ready to start a new chapter as a mother and honor Jack's memory in every way she could.

She headed back to the park to meet Miranda and her mother, the two had begun to get along as the prospect of being grandparents United them.

"Are you ready to leave?" Miranda asked. "Yes, let's go."

They all began to walk away from the park, she couldn't help but look into the sky, wondering what could have happened to her love.

Thank you for purchasing this book. If you enjoyed this book then please do not forget to rate it or leave a review or share it on social media. That would help me out greatly.

Made in the USA
Columbia, SC
20 September 2023

d40e0d1f-7606-4070-a861-bdf336bbce5dR01